Write Michigan 2021 Anthology

Chapbook Press

Chapbook Press
Schuler Books
2660 28th Street SE
Grand Rapids, MI 49512
(616) 942-7330
www.schulerbooks.com

ISBN 9781948237734

Benson Brazier   **Grace Jacobson**
Bailey Burke   **Lani Khuu**
Kevina Clear   **Abigail Kloha**
EF Coigne   **Karen McPhee**
Harper Davis   **Shelley Ouyang**
Susie Finkbeiner   **Anja Phillips**
Emerson Gerard   **Alivia Schnakenberg**
Lucio Gunckel   **Lillian Stielstra**
Hannah Haines   **Liene Strautnieks**
Cailynn Hamilton   **Andrew Wright**
Ellie Hardy   **Kate Zalapi-Bull**
Ariella Hillary   **Zack Zupin**
Xavier Irizarry

Printed in the United States by Chapbook Press.

Table of Contents

Foreword

Of Birds and Writers
Susie Finkbeiner

There was a time when I wasn't a woman who feeds birds. In those days, before I knew what suet and nyjer seeds were, I hardly ever thought of the birds in my neighborhood. Sure, occasionally I saw a big bird flying over head or a bunch of weird speckled birds swarming the lawn. But, for the most part, I went on with my life like a normal, non-birdfeeding individual.

Then one day on my way to the cat food aisle at the grocery store I wandered into the wild birdseed section.

"Huh. Why not?" I thought, and picked out a green plastic feeder (the cheapest on the shelf) and a five pound bag of seed.

Once home I hung my offering from a thick limb of our crimson maple. For days I watched eagerly, hoping for be-feathered diners to visit.

Imagine my pout when none came. Not a single one.

Turning to Google—as one does—I discovered the "Rule of Two". Essentially, this rule informs that it could take "Two seconds, two minutes, two hours, two days, two weeks, or two months"[1] for birds to make an appearance at a new feeder.

Welp. At least it didn't say the birds would never come.

I hunkered down and kept my eyes open.

My first bird—at least that I saw—was a sparrow. I'm certain that no other sparrow in the history of birdwatching was ever as celebrated as that one.

"You came!" I yelled, startling the birdie and sending it to flight.

Not to worry, my shouting did little to keep the birds away that day. They came steadily and I tried to identify them as best as I could.

The sparrows I knew and the robins. Any Michigander worth her salt knows a robin when she sees one. A noisy bluejay squawked when he arrived followed by a cardinal pair who made a much quieter entrance.

"These are my bird friends," I thought. "And they eat a lot."

After a few days I peeked out and found a different kind of avian in the

---

1. Thanks to The Zen Birdfeeder at Wild Birds Unlimited for this insight https:// wildbirdsunlimited.typepad.com/the_zen_birdfeeder/2011/03/hanging-new-birdfeeder- rule-of-twos.html

tree. It was blue and black and white and absolutely adorable. Like nothing I'd ever seen before. Then a black and white striped, jittery little guy. Then a rather Rubenesque trio. Next, one with silvery gray coloration and a punk rock mohawk.

"Who are these guys?" I wondered aloud. "And what do they like to eat?"

Did you know that there's an app that helps you identify birds? There is. Of course, there's an app for everything these days. But I digress.

I identified the nuthatch and downy woodpecker, the mourning doves and the tufted titmouse. As new birds came, I learned their names and kept that feeder full.

Eventually I branched out, offering thistle to try to attract a charm of goldfinches. Suet cake to lure in woodpeckers. Black-oil sunflower seeds to appeal to chickadees and grackles. I even put out mealworms, cringing the whole time.

Some of it the birds liked. Some of it they didn't, nudging it out of the way so they could reach the good stuff. All of it, however, was to the liking of the neighborhood squirrels. All of it they would steal.

Even full cakes of suet.

If you've never had the pleasure of watching a squirrel bolt across the street with a full suet cake in its mouth, let me tell you, you're missing out.

Also not to be missed is me, dashing out the front door to chase away Buttons the murderous neighborhood cat so he doesn't eat my house finches. It is, indeed, a sight to see.

Another digression. I apologize.

Over the years I've eased into the rhythm of being a bird nerd. I no longer buy seed in five pound bags, but in much heavier quantities. I keep an eye open for orioles and hummingbirds in the summer, juncos and Coopers hawks when the weather turns colder. I might talk to the nuthatch who no longer flies away when I come outside and I always answer when the bluejay hollers at me to let me know the feeder is empty.

I've learned to offer what I have and to delight in the birds that come.

It's not all that different from what we, as writers, come to learn over time.

One day we get an itch of an idea and think to ourselves, "Huh. Why not?" We grab our paper and pen or power-up the laptop and write a sentence. Then another and another.

Some of that first try is good. Some of it, a little rough. That's all right. We're trying something new and that takes a lot of courage. We write, edit, revise. Repeat.

After awhile we offer what we've written, hoping someone will come along to read it.

It might take two days, weeks, months, years, or even more before an eager reader finds our poem, story, essay, memoir. But when they do it is so exciting. And nerve-raking. But mostly exciting.

"You came!" we yell.

Then proceed to bite our nails to the quick.

We give what we can, we writers do. And even though what we offer might not be for everyone, it is for someone.

At first that someone might be our best friend from first grade or an especially inspiring teacher. It might even be our mom. But a reader is a reader.

And a writer is a writer. We just can't help ourselves.

While we wait for more readers to come, we keep tapping away at the keyboard or scribbling in our notebook. We try new things and stretch our writing muscles.

Eventually we come to realize that, while writing is a cathartic exercise for ourselves, it is also a gift to those who read it. A gift that nurtures, inspires, impacts, and nourishes.

We fill the world with words that speak of what it is to be human, to love, to despair, to suffer, to hope.

The pages of this chapbook are filled with the offerings of authors from across the State of Michigan. I, for one, am so proud of all the brave writers who submitted their work for the Write Michigan Short Story Contest.

To those whose stories didn't end up in this book, I beg of you not to give up. There are readers for you, readers who need what only you can write.

To the authors who are featured here, hearty and loud congratulations! I sincerely hope that the first thing you did when you received this chapbook was to flip through until you found your story. There's nothing like that moment, seeing what you've written in print. Relish it. Never let it get old. It's as close to magic as we get in this writing life.

To the readers, we hope you enjoy this feast—far better fare than anything set out for birds. It is, in fact, the best we can offer.

What delight to share it with you.

About the Author

Susie Finkbeiner is the award winning, bestselling author of *The Nature of Small Birds* as well as *All Manner of Things*, which was selected as a *2020 Michigan Notable Book*, and *Stories That Bind Us*. Susie and her husband have three children and live in West Michigan.

Adult Judges' Choice Winner

Forever Things
Karen McPhee

Kerry sat at her desk and looked out at the empty classroom. Just minutes before, 24 third graders had filled the worn and aging space with non-stop chatter and Tigger-like energy as they waited for the bell to sound, signaling the end of another school day and their release from captivity. They were gone in a chaotic burst, but Kerry could still feel their vivacity and smell the earthy sweat they had worked up during a late-afternoon recess. She smiled thinking about how Louie, the school's janitor of some 20-odd years, would lightly scold her as he cleaned up the crumbs of Goldfish crackers scattered across the landscape. She handed them out all afternoon to keep her students' energy up and their attention focused on equivalent fractions. In her heart, she knew Louie appreciated the extra care with which she tended her unruly flock even as he complained about the "Goldfish glitter."

For ten years, since her first day as a teacher, Kerry had been assigned to this classroom in one of the city's oldest schools in one of its poorest neighborhoods. It had been an atypical choice for a young woman who had grown up in the suburbs and attended top rated schools; their gleaming buildings stockpiled with all the possibilities and potential any student could ever need. But Kerry knew, from her short stint as a student teacher in this inner-city district, many of the glossy opportunities that had been available to her as a suburban student were painfully and persistently out of reach for students here. She wanted to make a difference. Maybe, she had reasoned, she could pack up some of that possibility and bring it with her every day.

So much had changed, though, during those ten years. Schools in general, and teachers specifically, had come under constant attack from warring political ideologies that demonstrated little understanding of the realities of teaching children, especially children who were becoming poorer, more transient, and less secure in all the things Maslow had defined as basic needs for survival in his famous Hierarchy. Adding to the political discontent was the increasing number of parents who would publicly and aggressively criticize teachers for failing their children when, oftentimes, it was society itself that had pulled up short. Then there were the deepening challenges of the students themselves. Social and emotional skills were increasingly void in the students she was seeing, and those deficiencies were at times playing out in aggressive behaviors that robbed other students of their education as distracted teachers managed the disruptions. The sum toll of it all was exacerbated in an inner-city school.

While third graders, in general, were optimistic cauldrons of pure human energy, Kerry had also witnessed a change in her eight-year-old charges. Some bore the scars of constant upheaval in their home lives, interfering with their ability to attach to their classmates and settle in to learn. For the past three years, her classroom transiency rate had hit 75 percent. Of the two dozen students who warmly greeted her on the first sweltering day of the new year in August, just six would still be in her classroom ten months later to hug her good-bye before scampering off on summer break. One by one, throughout the year, the other 18 students had moved somewhere else, sometimes with no warning and no forwarding address. One by one, new transient students had taken their places. Sometimes twice.

Kerry breathed in and out deeply as she surveyed the cacophony of desks before her, each a landing pad for a little human spirit. She bit her lower lip, choking back tears. She loved these students. She loved teaching. But she had made a heart-rending decision. In ten minutes she would meet with the Principal, Mark Green, and tell him she intended to resign at the end of the year; a decision she could not have fathomed just a few short months ago.

The notion she should leave teaching took up residence along the outer banks of her consciousness at the beginning of the school year when Kerry learned three of her colleagues had quit over the summer. The notion gained a foothold and then picked up steam as a particularly tough year unfolded. Fifteen of her students had left during the year; the revolving door ushering in a new student to fill each empty seat. Two students had lost parents to drug overdoses. Her students had worked so hard to learn the mechanics of reading, writing, and basic math; yet she knew many would fall short on the standardized tests she had just administered. There just hadn't been enough time to get them all ready. There was never enough time. Each tragic turn of events, as she saw them now, was mounting evidence for her self-indictment. She was failing her students. She was failing their future. They deserved better. She would go.

Kerry reached into the top drawer of her desk and retrieved the letter she had written days before, the one formalizing her decision and putting the district on notice this year would be her last. She glanced at the clock and knew she needed to head to Mark's office. She had asked for this meeting and he would be waiting for her.

Kerry walked out into the deserted hallway which, just moments earlier, had been a noisy traffic jam of students, staff, and parents. The long corridor was now dark; the closed doors of the classrooms it connected denying it direct sunlight except at the very end where it met the large glass entryway heading outside to the parking lot. The late afternoon sun lit that terminus portal now with an almost ethereal light, a beacon at the end of a dark tunnel. Kerry walked toward the light and Mark's office which sat just inside the glowing doors.

As she made her way down the hall, a human figure appeared in the illuminated entrance.

The person appeared almost to be an apparition, washed in both darkness and light, sun and shadow. She wasn't even sure if it was a man or a woman until the specter came further into the hallway and the searing backlight was tempered by the dim aging florescent bulbs humming overhead. It was a young man. Probably someone's father. Probably late picking up his son or daughter.

She had almost walked by him when he spoke. "Miss Simms?" Kerry was surprised to hear her name. "Yes. And you are?"

"It's Jamal Salib, Miss Simms. You were my third-grade teacher."

§

Kerry was stunned. The young man standing before her bore little resemblance to the gaunt young boy who had shown up in her classroom ten years earlier, two months after school had started, struggling with English, withdrawn and frightened. It was her first year teaching. It was Jamal's first year in America as a Syrian refugee. He, his parents, and four siblings had fled their war-torn country and had been relocated to the city by an international humanitarian organization. It might have been ten years and hundreds of students ago, but Kerry remembered her year with Jamal in vivid detail.

As any self-aware teacher will eventually admit, first year teachers have a lot to learn and much of that learning comes in the form of on-the-job training and trial and error. Colleges might produce the necessary paper credentials, but it's experience that produces effective and successful teachers. Jamal would have presented challenges to even a seasoned veteran.

Fortunately for him, Kerry was in her first year of teaching and blissfully naïve, unaware that success wasn't a guarantee.

First, there was the language barrier. While the agency that sponsored their relocation was working with the entire Salib family to improve their language skills, Kerry knew it was imperative she speed up Jamal's transition from his native Arabic to English. She scoured the Internet for translation resources and began working with Jamal during recesses, lunch periods, and after school to accelerate his command of the language. Fortunately, Jamal was like a human sponge, quickly soaking up every word, phrase, colloquialism, and slang term he would need to master reading, the gateway to all other learning.

Kerry knew, from conversations with his mother and his community advocate, Jamal had witnessed more death and suffering in his short life than most of his new contemporaries would experience in their lifetimes. She knew she had to be patient while he adjusted to his new reality and she felt an almost maternal instinct to protect him from any other form of pain. He was, at first, quiet and withdrawn, a cautious loner. But slowly, over time, as his command of the language and his understanding of American culture grew, and his brilliant mind emerged, he blossomed right in front of her, like a sunflower turning its gape to the nourishing sun. By the end of that year, he was on pace to be one of the most competent students in her class. His early stoicism gave way to a warm and infectious confidence. The other students, as third graders are apt to do, quickly followed their emergent leader. Having no other experience with which to judge it against, Kerry merely thought she had done well by Jamal that first year. He moved on to fourth grade. She lost track of him.

"Jamal. Of course. It's so good to see you. How are you? What are you doing here?" Kerry asked with genuine curiosity.

Jamal responded as if it should have been obvious. "Why I'm here to see you, Miss Simms."

While he was certainly a young man now, some of the boyish charms persisted. Absent the sun-induced shroud, she could now see his piercing dark eyes and the small L-shaped scar on his forehead which she had never asked him about and the mop of inky black hair that curled haphazardly around his face.

"You're here to see me? What can I do for you, Jamal?"

"Miss Simms I'm graduating next month, and I just found out I will finish in the top ten of my class."

"Jamal that's wonderful! I'm so proud of you!" Kerry was not surprised but genuinely thrilled that this former protégé had continued to excel.

Jamal continued. "I have a favor to ask. The district puts on a lunch for the top ten students and their families. Each student gets to invite one teacher to the lunch...the teacher who had the most impact on their success in school. Miss Simms, I would like to invite you."

Kerry stood speechless. Emotion seized the back of her throat. Her eyes began to moisten. How could Jamal think she had had the most impact on his success in school. Surely there were high school teachers who had introduced him to exciting new areas of study and engaged him in extra-curricular activities that expanded his understanding of the world and his place in it. By contrast, what had she done? Taught him the life cycle of a tomato plant? And what would those high school teachers say when an elementary teacher showed up at an honors event. It was an unwritten rule that graduation and its associated pomp and circumstance were the sole purview of high schools. Elementary school teachers were not expected to be a part of those events, as if somehow what happened in the earlier grades was irrelevant to a student's later success.

§

"Jamal, I...I don't know what to say. I'm so honored but I honestly have to ask. Why me? We haven't seen each other in almost ten years. Surely you've had other teachers who've made an impact on you."

Jamal smiled. "Of course I have, Miss Simms, but if it hadn't been for you, I'm not sure I would have made it out of grade school, much less graduate at the top of my class. It might have been a long time ago, but I remember everything from that first year like it was yesterday. You taught me how to speak English. You protected me from students who didn't understand where I had come from, why I looked and sounded different. You treated me with respect, expected me to do my best, and you made me believe I was smart. I was so scared for so long and then I got to your classroom, Miss Simms, and it was the first time in my life I can remember feeling safe outside of my own home. You gave me hope that it would all be OK. That I would be OK."

The tears were now running down Kerry's cheeks. Could an eight-year-old boy really have been that self-aware? "Oh my, Jamal. Of course I'll attend the luncheon as your guest. It will be the honor of my lifetime. Just let me know when and where."

Jamal's smile widened in appreciation. "Thank you, Miss Simms. I was hoping you'd say yes. I know it's been a long time, but the things I learned from you? Well, Miss Simms, those are the forever things. I'll never be able to thank you enough."

Kerry could only smile and nod her head, the overwhelming rush of emotion catching her words in her throat. Forever things? She imagined he meant confidence and curiosity and work ethic and the self-agency to foster continual forward motion. Things teachers teach without literal intent or lesson plans. Things standardized tests didn't measure.

Jamal was turning to leave. "I have to get going, though. I'm picking up my little sister from her piano lesson and then I need to study for a test. I'll send you the official invitation with all the details." Jamal headed back toward the luminous glow of the doorway just ahead.

"Perfect, Jamal. And thank you. You have no idea what this means to me."

And much like he had arrived, Jamal slipped out the door into a wash of bright light.

Kerry watched his form disappear into the universe beyond the glass threshold. She bit her lower lip as the tears continued to dance down her cheeks. Jamal seemed like eons ago and just seconds before. While the staccato cadence of a school year offers teachers short-term evidence of their impact on student learning, rarely do teachers get to ponder the long game. But there it was. The long game. Jamal. Then the truth encased her like a slow embrace. Jamal had been a transient student. Jamal had harbored deep emotional scars. Jamal required extra time and attention to give him even the remotest chance of coming up even. That he excelled was not so much the miracle. The miracle was she didn't see herself as a part of it, until now. How many other students like Jamal had there been? How many other students like Jamal were yet destined for her classroom?

Kerry smiled and shook her head, acknowledging the razor thin line that often dances between the cosmos and chaos, where unexpected events experienced in the always fleeting seconds of the here and now can interrupt and redirect one's long term outlook and direction. She walked toward the same light that had just swallowed Jamal whole. As she passed his office, Mark Green saw her and stepped out into the hallway.

"Kerry? Don't we have a meeting?"

Kerry stopped and turned to face him. "I'm so sorry, Mark. If you don't mind, I'd like to cancel our meeting."

"No problem," Mark answered. "Mind if I ask what kinds of things were on your mind?" "Why, forever things, Mark. Forever things."

And with that, Kerry followed Jamal into the light.

Mark walked back into his office, relief washing over him as he thought back to how it all started. He and Kerry began teaching at the school on the same day ten years earlier. Their friendship was born of their mutual naivete as novice teachers and their disparate personal realities. She was from the suburbs. He was from the neighborhood. She had no interest in becoming a principal. He aspired to lead. They had buoyed each other through a decade's worth of challenges and triumphs. Mark always assumed their professional partnership would last forever, or at least until they both decided to hang it up another two decades down the road.

When Kerry talked to him yesterday morning and asked to set up a meeting, he was afraid he knew why. He knew this had been a tougher than normal year for Kerry. He had watched her confidence deflate as the year's struggles mounted. He had tried to bolster her resolve, but the look in her eyes and the defeat in her voice told him he had not done enough. She had wanted to meet yesterday after school, but he already had a principals meeting scheduled at the high school and asked if it could wait till today. She had agreed.

He was running late for that meeting at the high school yesterday when, head down and moving fast, he literally ran into Jamal as he rounded a turn in the hallway. After laughing off the collision, the two recognized each other and spent a few minutes catching up. Mark was now the principal at Jamal's former grade school. Jamal would soon be graduating with top honors. Mark congratulated Jamal on his success. Jamal thanked Mark for everything he and the teachers at his former school had done to make sure he succeeded, especially his first teacher, Miss Simms.

Then the universe tilted ever so slightly in the direction of hope by offering Mark a reminder that forever can be built by harnessing the potential of each moment at hand before it evaporates into the next, casting the course of our hours, days, years.

Jamal simply said "If there's anything I can ever do..."

About the Author

Karen McPhee fell in love with writing when her fourth-grade teacher taught her how to diagram sentences while encouraging her to think of words as paint on canvas. Her career included six-years as a television news journalist and 35 years in education, as a communications director, superintendent, education policy director, and strategic planning consultant. Now retired, she lives in West Michigan with her husband Marty and enjoys traveling, hiking, and photography. She's two thirds of the way through writing her first novel, which she hopes to finish sometime this decade.

Adult Judges' Choice Runner-Up
Dahlia
Liene Strautnieks

She was lying on a frozen bed of grass, the outline of trees blurry in front of her. Her mouth tasted like a rusty spoon and it felt like a dagger was piercing her abdomen with every inhale. Their fists and feet had been relentless, unforgiving. Her thighs were chilled where her gown was torn, and her ankle was in agony. But none of this compared to the torment between her legs. Dahlia parted her bloated, bloodied lips to yell for help, but words did not come. She clenched her teeth together to keep them from chattering, the air feeling like hundreds of tiny needles pricking her skin. Her jaw trembled before fresh, hot salt spilled down her cheek. Then everything went black.

A whiff of antiseptic and the warmth of sunlight forced Dahlia's eyes open. Her ankle was cradled in a cast and there was an ice pad laying against her ribs. Her eyes shifted to her inner right arm where a tube stuck into her skin, connected to a plastic bag hanging next to her. There was a contraption on her nose and bandage wrapped around her head. But the worst pain was between her legs – a physical reminder that she was still a he. Dahlia heard a knock at the door, followed by a middle-aged woman in aqua scrubs.

"Well, good morning," the woman said, her voice melodic. "I'm glad to see you're awake." Dahlia blinked at her.

"Do you know where you are?"

"Hospital?" Dahlia asked. Her voice felt like sandpaper.

"Yes, you're at Metro Health. Your friend Bethany called the ambulance. You were admitted last night and have been out for almost 12 hours. Can you tell me your full name?"

Dahlia swallowed, turning to look at the nurse's name tag – Nina, RN.

"Dalmiro Jesús Malter," Dahlia said, the r's rolling off her tongue.

"Good," Nina said, adjusting Dahlia's pillow. "What's your date of birth, Dalmiro?"

"July 6th, 1993. Um –" Dahlia started, then hesitated. "Can you please call me Dahlia?" She closed her eyes so she couldn't see Nina's judgment. There was a pause.

"Of course. What a beautiful name," Nina said, putting a hand on Dahlia's shoulder.

Dahlia opened her eyes, several emotions sliding down her cheeks.

Nina smiled behind her turtle shell specs, rubbing Dahlia's arm. "Alright, I'm going to make a couple notes in your chart about your name for any future visits, ok?"

Dahlia nodded against the pillow, a thought occurring to her. "Please don't tell my parents."

"I won't," Nina said. "That's confidential. Your parents are in the cafeteria grabbing some breakfast. They'll be back shortly. Your friend called them last night, and they came as soon as they heard. Your mom didn't sleep a wink. I –" Nina's voice trailed off as Dahlia fixated on her words – didn't sleep a wink. Wink. Alex winked at me. Her heart began thumping in her chest, thoughts racing.

Dahlia stood with Bethany, her best friend since 4th grade, up against the wall of the hotel ballroom, swinging her hips to the beat. It was the first time she had dressed like a girl in public – wig, makeup, gown, and her first ever pair of heels. Bethany had helped Dahlia get ready at Beth's parent's house. The entire senior class was catching flies in their mouths when she and Beth had first arrived. She was surprised how many compliments and support she had received, especially from the teacher chaperones. More importantly, Alex Chapman had noticed.

Alex was the captain of the swim team, and her biggest crush since 7th grade, when he had lent her a pen in history class and she had noticed how soft and coppery his eyes were. He was standing now with his swim team pals on the other side of the room. They were exchanging something. She watched Alex shove something into his pocket, turn, and shuffle his way back onto the dance floor. He was grinding up against their class president, Amy. Dahlia imagined what it would feel like to have Alex's body pressed up against her own. She thought back to a few months prior, when she had found Alex pressed up against the toilet, puking at a swim team party. Beth was dating Johnny, their best freestyle swimmer, so she had invited Dalmiro.

"You ok in there?" Dalmiro asked, opening the bathroom door, peeking in.

"M' fine," Alex mumbled against the porcelain. Dalmiro came in, shutting the door behind him. He walked over and knelt next to Alex. Without thinking, his hand started sliding up and down Alex's back. Alex lifted his head off the seat, rocking a bit.

"Thanks," he said. His breath smelled sour. Alex's hand found its way onto Dalmiro's knee. It rested there for a moment, then he began stroking Dalmiro's thigh under his skin-tight Gap jeans. Dalmiro stared at Alex's hand, then met his bloodshot eyes. Alex leaned in, but Dalmiro pulled back.

"S' matter? Don' you like kissin' boys?" He slurred.

"Alex, you're drunk. And your mouth is kind of pukey," Dalmiro said, scrunching his face. Alex wiped his face on his sleeve.

"Yerright. M' sorry." He half-fell into Dalmiro's arms, head rolling into Dalmiro's shoulder, eyes closed. "Next time," he mumbled. Dalmiro smiled into Alex's hair that smelled like fresh rain, holding him and rubbing his back until Beth found them and they helped him to bed. Dahlia hadn't heard a word from Alex since, but his words kept her up at night. Next time.

"How is your pain, Dahlia?"

Nina's voice startled her. She twitched. "Sorry, what?" Dahlia asked.

"How's your pain?"

"Um, 5 or 6," she said.

"Ok, I'll grab some more tramadol and let the doctor know you're awake. Just use the buzzer if you need something, ok? I'll be right back."

"Thank you," Dahlia said. Nina left the room and Dahlia turned to look at the morning sun coming through the blinds, thinking back to the dance. That moment. Alex.

"I'm gonna go grab some punch. Want some?" Beth asked, interrupting Dahlia's thoughts.

"Sure, thanks," Dahlia smiled. Beth took off towards the refreshments. When she was gone, Dahlia looked up, locking eyes with Alex as Lady Gaga's "Judas" came through the speakers.

Oh, oh, oh, oh, oh.

I'm in love with Judas, Judaas.

That's when Alex's right eye winked, his lips pulling into his slender cheek, smirking. Dahlia stopped dancing, her stomach cartwheeling. She turned and peered over her shoulder, knowing there'd been a mistake, but behind her was just a wall of scattered balloons and blinking lights. She looked back to see that he had moved away from Amy and was dancing on his own, eyes still locked on hers.

Forgive him when his tongue lies through his brain Even after three times he betrays me.

She smiled back, shifting her weight from one heel to the other, giving a half wave. He signaled for her to join him on the dance floor. She could feel her heartbeat in her throat.

"Here we go," Nina said, entering the room. The sensual memory dissipated into the sterile air and vanquished. Dahlia watched as Nina changed her IV bag. She felt a cold flush in her arm when Nina administered the medication. Dahlia shivered. Nina grabbed another blanket and draped it over Dahlia's midsection. Dahlia smiled, thankful. Dahlia could feel the pulse in her throat.

Her parents would be back any moment. My dad's gonna kill me.

"I'm not going unless I can wear a dress," Dahlia protested, crossing her arms. "It's my prom, I should be able to wear what I want."

"You're goin' to your goddamn senior prom whether you like it or not, and you're gonna wear a fuckin' tuxedo because that's what guys wear," her father said, rising from his armchair, smashing his empty Heineken to the floor. "It's bad enough we gotta deal with you wearing tight pants and girly fuckin' shirts all the time, acting like such a little fag."

Dennis Malter had always been quick to anger. Dahlia and her mother, Catalina, had often felt his wrath, emotionally or otherwise. If either one pissed him off enough, he would make his mark and shut them up. He had slapped Dahlia so hard after she had come out as being gay a few years earlier, that she couldn't go to school for three days due to the bruising. They had barely spoken since.

Dahlia turned to her mother, eyes begging to say something in Dahlia's defense, but her mother pursed her lips together and shrugged.

"You will look so handsome in a tux, mijo," she said softly. She gave Dahlia a quick kiss on the forehead, then turned to retrieve the broom out of the pantry.

"Aye, que guapo!" Catalina beamed a few weeks later as Dahlia came down the steps in a black Calvin Klein tuxedo with an amethyst bow tie and matching vest. It felt like a potato sack. At least her hair was long enough to pull into a bun.

"Let me get my camera," her mother said. Dennis was sitting in front of the TV watching the Lions, five empty bottles tossed all over the floor.

"Let's go outside," she said, ushering Dahlia out the door. "Ooh, that's chilly," she said, the cool, March breeze floating into the house. "Dennis, do you want to be in a few photos?"

Dennis didn't take his eyes off the television, shaking his head as if she'd asked him if he had changed the lightbulb yet at the top of the stairs. Catalina frowned, then stepped onto the front stoop, camera ready.

"Ok mamá!" Dahlia groaned, wiggling her toes in her shoes. "I'm going to be late." "Ok, ok," Catalina said half-apologetically. "You just look so handsome!"

Dahlia sighed. She wanted to be called 'pretty' or 'beautiful.' 'Handsome' made her feel masculine, confined. She went back into the house, grabbed the keys, and started for the door.

Dennis hadn't bothered to say a word as she crossed the threshold.

Dahlia gave her mom a wave, pulling away from the curb, feeling guilty. Catalina had paid to rent the tux she was wearing, but little did she know that Dahlia was on her way to Beth's house to change into a sequin gown from JCPenney, put on a brown, wavy wig Beth had from Halloween, and finish with a bit of glossy lip.

Dahlia was moving without thinking towards Alex onto the dance floor. The music was muffled, a blurry filter on the scene. Alex was the only thing in focus.

"So, Dalmiro," Alex said over the lyrics, "dresses huh?" "First time, actually," she said.

"Pretty ballsy," he said. "You don't look half bad as a girl." Dahlia blushed.

"Thanks," she said, smelling his Axe body spray mixed with sweat. "I've felt like one for a while."

It was the only time she had said it aloud to anyone besides Beth. It felt good. Alex stopped dancing. So did Dahlia. Had she said something wrong? They stood still among the swaying crowd looking at one another. Finally, Alex leaned in, lips barely grazing her ear.

"Let's get some air," he said. Dahlia gulped at his closeness. She pulled away, face hot.

Before she could respond, his clammy hand wrapped around hers, dragging her towards the door. He looked over his shoulder as they went, as if checking for something.

"Where are we going?" Dahlia asked. They hadn't stopped in the parking lot.

"We need some privacy," he said, moving towards the woods. Dahlia had forgotten how to breathe. A million thoughts raced in her mind, her heels clicking on the pavement. Was this 'next time'? He walked another fifty yards, entering the edge of the trees. She followed him, the ground hard enough that her heels didn't sink into the snowy soil.

"So, did you want to talk or -?" Dahlia asked.

"Actually, I'm hoping you'll share with me," he said, whipping out a pint of Jack Daniels from inside his coat.

"Oh," Dahlia said, surprised. "Um, sure."

He unclasped the top, took a huge swig, mouth puckering, then handed her the bottle. The booze burned her throat, making her hack.

"Wow!" She said, eyes watering.

"Right? This stuff gets you super wasted."

"Like last time?" She asked. He took the bottle from her, looking at the ground.

"Yeah, about that," he began, "I wanted to, uh, thank you. You know, for taking care of me at Robbie's."

"You're welcome. I wasn't sure you even remembered that night."

"I remembered you," he said, a new glow in his eyes. There was a long stillness in the air between them.

"Come here," he said, setting the bottle down. Dahlia moved toward him. His hands found her hip bones. "You can't tell anyone about that night."

"I won't," she whispered, taking in the warmth of him.

"And you can't tell anyone about this either," he said, leaning in and planting his boozy lips on hers. She melted into his mouth, feeling his lips part and then come back down. She could feel herself getting hard underneath the pantyhose. The moment lasted only seconds, but it felt like a forever she never wanted to end.

"Holy shit, he really did it!" Came a voice from behind them. Dahlia looked up, bewildered and saw three figures approaching. It was Robbie, Dane, and Zac – Alex's swim team buddies. Alex pulled away, his eyes wild. He wiped his mouth on his suit coat sleeve and spit on the ground.

"Where the fuck have you guys been?" He asked. "I told you to count to ten, then follow me out. Were you dicks waiting for me to bend him over or what?"

"Sorry man, we thought you might hear us if we followed too close," Robbie said. "What's going on?" Dahlia asked, hearing the panic in her voice.

"You got played, you little fag," Zac sneered. "We told Alex we'd give him thirty bucks if he got you to kiss him tonight."

Dahlia looked at Alex. His eyes were lost and frightened.

"Dude, I cannot believe you actually did it! Totally worth it the money," Dane said. "Hell yeah, man," Zac echoed, the two guys high fiving each other.

Alex picked the bottle back up, drank his uncomfortability, and turned to leave. "You guys are assholes," Dahlia said, tears sliding down her rosy cheeks.

"Aww, did we upset the little fairy queen?" Zac asked, running his fingers down his cheeks, mocking her tears.

"I thought after you rubbed my leg in the bathroom that night –" Dahlia started, but Alex turned and threw the bottle against a nearby tree, interrupting her, the amber liquid splattering them.

"Shut up!" He said.

"You said next time," Dahlia said. "What did that mean, then?" "What's he talking about, Alex?" Zac asked.

"Nothing!" Alex said, his voice going up. "He's making shit up!"

"You tried to kiss me at Robbie's," Dahlia said. Everything went still. No one moved or spoke. The only sounds that came were the wind and everyone's breathing.

"You're lying!" Alex finally said.

"Dude, is that true?" Robbie asked, mortified. "No! I –" Alex fumbled.

"It is true! Stop lying, Alex!" Dahlia said.

"Shut the fuck up you stupid faggot!" Alex yelled. His fist came flying into her face so fast she did not have time to react. His knuckles smashed her nose, making her head slam into the tree. There was a sudden flurry of dizziness.

The world spun and she toppled over, landing on her side. Alex sent another fist into her face from above, his buddies joining in soon after. Their punches. Their black soles. Their relentless hatred.

But he had liked it, hadn't he? Dahlia thought. She had heard him groan softly when his lips had been on hers. She felt something in her left ankle snap. They smashed their toes between her legs, the several pairs of pantyhose unable to shield her. How had it come to this? They had been dancing and kissing just moments before. Was there ever really going to be a 'next time', like he had said? Alex's hatred was a mask, she decided. A mask for everything he wished he never was or never would be.

After several minutes, the pummeling stopped. The voices died away as pain consumed her. She stared after them, but all she could see was a hazy outline of trees. She lay shivering, realizing no one would find her until she was frozen. A numbness took over her. The world faded to black, and her head hit the ground with a thud.

There was a knock at the door. Dahlia turned and saw Catalina and Dennis enter the room.

"Mijo," Catalina said, rushing to her son, hugging him and kissing him where he wasn't bandaged. "Estoy aquí."

"I – I'm sorry," Dahlia sobbed, holding her mother. She knew her father was towering over them and did not want to look up to see the disgust and disappointment on his face.

"Oh, mijo," Catalina said through tears of her own. "I'm sorry. Perdóname, mi amor.

Perdóname."

"At least the little shit who did this to you got what he deserved," Dennis finally said. "Not now, Dennis," Catalina said.

"What do you mean?" Dahlia asked.

"That Alex kid killed himself last night. Got an email from the school. Hung himself, I guess."

There were words that came after that, but Dahlia could not comprehend them. She stared blankly ahead, unable to make sense of the muffled, incoherent sounds that were coming from Dennis's mouth. They were like severing a delicate stem, leaving the blossom to wilt and wither into a new darkness.

"Dalmiro," Dennis said. Dahlia continued staring forward. "Dalmiro?" Dennis said again. His tone was foreign to her.

Dahlia looked up and met his gaze. They looked at one another in silence. She studied his face but couldn't understand what his expression meant. She had never seen it before.

About the Author

Liene is a Grand Rapids, Michigan native who has always had a passion for reading and writing. She enjoyed writing poetry in her adolescent years, but when she went to Aquinas College to receive her Bachelor of Arts in Theatre, writing fell to the wayside and theatre became a larger part of her life. Now, in her early thirties, Liene is thrilled to say that she has finally started writing again. "Dahlia" is Liene's first ever short story and submission to any contest or competition. She is blessed and honored to have had her story selected as a semifinalist in the Write Michigan event series. Liene is a proud member of the LGBTQIA+ community and resides in Grand Rapids with her best friend and wife, Patti. They have been together for 17+ years.

Adult Readers' Choice Winner
Dark Lord Sounds A Bit Harsh, Don't You Think?
Benson Brazier

I knew that another one was coming, I could hear the sounds of battle even up in my study. Despite my warnings and the constant safety meetings, my overprotective minions insisted on challenging these heroes. I would have prefered a clearly marked path straight to me, but my generals wouldn't allow it. I tried to explain that it would be easier than sending the constant condolence letters home to the families of the fallen, but their honor demanded that they protect me. They rationalized it as trying to allow me to focus on my mission, but in truth even the best of them were a stalling tactic; the heroes were too strong to be stopped by anything short of true power.

I straightened up my desk before heading down to the workshop to confront the hero's inevitable dramatic entrance. Ten years ago I had ordered all the heavy doors of the keep replaced by cheap wooden ones to save on replacements after whatever muscular companion the hero had allied themself with invariably came crashing through. I had also ordered that all vents and dumbwaiters in the tower be replaced with smaller high efficiency units or filled in altogether. It cut down on headaches now that I knew the hero would be coming in through the door rather than underfoot or overhead.

The Dark Lord before me had clearly been a theater major early in life because he had built the tower with huge gothic ceiling arches that cast the entire room into shadows so deep that literally anyone could hide in them. And now the so-called 'Great and the Good' were sending in a variety of heroes. At first it had been the classic champions—Princelings with more smoldering charm than brains; Knights with glowing swords large enough to compensate for their ... shortcomings; and generic warriors out to avenge a loved one that my predecessor had killed, bewitched, or kept captive in his comically insecure dungeons.

§

Now, however, the Great and the Good were sending halflings with invisibility cloaks, teeanagers who were just coming to terms with their latent magic powers and their even stronger hormones, young men who didn't know they were Princelings until I revealed their heritage to them, and Knights who were actually clever young women trying to win their right to self-determination. They were all decent sorts that I tried to spare and convince to come work for me instead, but centuries of brainwashing and propaganda from the Great and the Good had left them without the ability to see that simply believing that their cause was just didn't mean that they stood a chance against a vastly superior power.

And to that end, I mused as I magically unlocked the secret door that led into my elaborate workshop, it wasn't as if the Great and the Good were above cheating. Despite their pledge to not interfere in the lives of lesser beings and to protect the rights of man, they were now brazenly interfering in ways that definitely didn't protect anyone. The last hero they sent was wearing a magic ring so powerful that it was leaching his life away. And they call me a monster.

I opened the tap that poured the lava into the pit beneath the immense cauldron in the center of the room, into which I threw a formula that would start to bubble up in a sickly lime green color. When the room was prepared I threw my black cloak over my shoulders and picked up the staff with the red gem and horns on the end. The staff was perhaps too "bleeding heart" of me, it was surprisingly expensive to replace every time the hero broke it, but I liked them to feel like they accomplished something before they died. It, like nearly everything that I was activating in this room, was a holdover from my predecessor. I had absolutely no use for such trivial items, but I felt that I owed the heroes the comfort of the expected atrocities, to feel like their deaths were in service of the greater good. Whatever that was.

I sat on a stool at the back of the room and mentally contacted my chief of security. "General Culpa, are your cleanup crews ready?"

There was a momentary pause, "Uh, no my Lord. It would seem that this hero has a small army of companions. They assaulted the castle not just from the tunnels below as one would expect of adventurers, but they also sent in a division through the front door like heathens. The cleanup crews are still trying to put the entrance hall back together after their wizard decided to cast fireballs, as if he didn't know any other spells."

I sighed, "I understand. Please tell the troops to ignore the room, our primary goal is to get their bodies out of here as quickly as possible to prevent the Great and the Good from reanimating their bodies like they did with those poor kids last week. I don't think I could stomach having to kill them twice."

"Yes, m'lord." The poor man was actually a brilliant tactician and a force of nature with a battle-ax, but mopping up saddened him in a way that I wouldn't have expected from a former captain of the royal guard. Then again, the royal guard was far more savage than anything I was prepared to put forward.

The sounds of battle from below died out and I knew that their party must have defeated the last of the guards in the grand throne room one level down. That room was the size of a small town and the throne at the end was made of a fusion of skulls from more races than I could identify. It was old too, far older than my predecessor. Perhaps even older than this tower if some of the skulls on there were real. I never used it, it was too twisted even for me. Something about sitting on that throne began to fill you with the sort of thoughts that made building a throne like that seem logical. I didn't remove it though, because for one, an artifact like that might very well fight back, and for another it was a magnificent source of power to pull from for my work.

Any moment now the adventurers would stumble upon the secret stair in the wall behind the throne, and then they would be here. I looked around to make sure that everything was bubbling, fizzling, burning, or glowing as it should be to give the adventurers the dramatic scene they were so clearly expecting. I even activated the enchantment on the thin wooden door to make it look like it was actually steel, then I waited.

Sure enough, seconds later the door was transformed into a cloud of flying splinters and a motley crew of warriors came bursting into the room without so much as a witty greeting.

Perhaps I was becoming too much like my predecessor, but that annoyed me. After all the trouble I went through to make my home as comfortable a place to die as I could, they couldn't even be bothered to engage me in witty banter. Kids this century, I tell you.

The first through the door was some sort of half giant, a grotesque form of knotted muscles and disproportionately sized limbs. Clearly a great deal of magic had been used to enhance what was already an unfortunate hybrid. This poor female's face was a pitiable rictus of pain. Following her was a halfling whose dark clothes and artfully done eyeliner clearly indicated that he fancied himself a rogue. After that came four identical elven archers each holding an enchanted bow that would cost more than an entire village. I couldn't tell if they were clones, illusions, or just highly improbable quadruplets but I put them at the top of the Kill List before they could wreck my workshop with their doubtlessly explosive arrows.

§

After the elves came a portly human wizard dressed in robes so absurdly colorful that it would have made a peacock feel underdressed. He had his wand out and looked like he was indeed the sort who had only ever learned Fireball. I mentally put him at the top of the list and resolved to do something about the wizardry schools after I had finally finished with The Great and The Good.

The last to enter was a teenage boy with handsomely tousled hair, a crown-shaped birthmark on his forehead, and a sword that shone so brightly that it could have been a stage prop. He was glaring at me so intensely that I knew that he was going to accuse me of murdering his parents and/or his one true love.

The rest of his merry band spread out around the chamber to surround me, but oddly none of them spoke or even jeered. Instead they all silently waited, lending an air of gravitas to the situation that I am sure my predecessor would have relished.

Finally the boy spoke, his low voice full of malice, "Sorry to drop in unannounced, m'lord, but I thought we would make the end of your life an exciting surprise."

I was legitimately surprised; as bravado went that wasn't bad. Maybe this one would be worth bantering with after all.

I smiled indulgently, "So considerate of you. Please allow me to make you comfortable."

I casually waved my hand toward the wizard, causing the overdressed man to suddenly turn into a large grey rat. I wasn't going to hurt them before I could offer them the chance of a peaceful exit, but I also wasn't going to just let this idiot shoot off a bunch of fireballs like some monkey flinging its own feces.

I let the four arrows fired by the four elves bounce off of my cloak and didn't even turn to face them. "Be still," I said as pleasantly as I could. "Your companion is unharmed, though I dare say that he might receive some much-needed humbling from this experience. I just needed a chance to talk to you without him doing any unnecessary damage to my workshop."

"I think I can speak for all of us," the handsome boy with the crown-shaped birthmark said with a sneer, "when I say that we have no interest in anything you have to say, fiend. You are the great enemy of all the Free People and your life is forfeit."

"See, that is exactly what we need to talk about. Why am I your enemy? What have I done to you? Honestly, if you can name even one thing that I have done to any of you personally, then I will let you clamp iron shackles on me and I will come face whatever justice you deem appropriate."

"You ask for one, but I can give you many!" the boy exclaimed. "You cursed the land my village farms, which caused my adopted family to nearly starve. If the Great and the Good had not compensated them for allowing me to go on this quest they would have died."

I smiled gently, "I am truly sorry to hear of your suffering, but I have never cursed any land anywhere, let alone some farmland that never did anything to me. That sounds like a waste of considerable magic. What proof do you have that it was cursed and not simply a draught?"

The boy gave me a look of incredulity, "Why would the rain stop coming if not by your vile hand?"

"And what about my father?" The four elves said in unison, confirming my suspicions about being clones, "You lured him away from his family and used him for your sick experiments!"

"And when was that?" I asked.

"When I was a small child," replied the four voice chorus, "five hundred and seventy two years ago."

"That would be a good trick for me to pull, considering that I only took over this tower four hundred years ago. Besides, who said that I lured him away and that he didn't simply leave his family? Many fathers do."

The elves growled at me in unison, but the boy's frown was one of confusion. "Four hundred years ago? This tower has been a blight upon the land for more than a millennia. It is mentioned even before the founding of the Free Lands. No more of your lies, m'lord, I am not so easily deluded."

"I never thought you were. You seem quite bright to me, that is why I wanted to talk to you. To answer your question, yes, I usurped this tower's previous occupant a mere four hundred years ago. And he himself had only been its master for roughly a hundred years at that point. I have no idea who he stole the tower from or even who was the tower's original lord. I do, however, know that when you build your empire entirely on the fear of one man, it is best if you portray that man as a monolithic eternal entity, not as a series of men."

"So you spread this lie yourself to further your empire?" The dramatic looking halfling asked, having sidled up far closer to me than I had realized. "That makes you even more dishonorable than I thought."

"You misunderstand, my surprisingly stealthy friend," I said giving him an encouraging smile. "I do not have nor do I desire an empire. All I desire is peace and self-determination.

However, those things are incompatible with the desires of the Great and the Good. Those tyrants have bent the world to their will and nothing that disagrees with them is allowed to live.

When I was young, they took my older brother to fight in their wars. He was a kind soul who wanted nothing more than to tend to our father's farm. But they took him in shackles and he died with a stranger's sword in his belly. A stranger who himself was probably there against his will. When I protested against this, they arrested me, burned down our farm and scattered my family into the woods.

When I was freed I learned the arcane arts to fight back. The more I learned, the more they tried to stop me. That went on for a hundred years till I eventually took over this tower so I could work in peace without adventurers interrupting me daily. However, the Great and the Good cannot allow dissent to remain, so they sent better and better adventurers. In a way, they forced me to take on this dark lord persona. I went from a humble farmer to this, just to keep away from adventurers."

I laughed sadly at that realization, then stopped when I saw the disbelieving faces looking at me. "But I digress. I can see that my musings don't amuse you, so I will give you this one offer. Walk away. You can just walk away with your weapons and lives intact. No one will harass you on your way out. Or you could stay and join me, and you will be valued members of my forces. I will pay you, house you and your loved ones, and I will welcome your help in making a better world. Or you can die where you stand. I will take no satisfaction from it, but I cannot delay my work any longer.

So, what will it be? Your lives or your missguided mission?"

The group looked at each other, then everyone looked to the young man for guidance. He, however, never took his eyes off of me.

"My answer is, LIGHTNING STRIKE." He shouted as he threw out his hand and shot a lightning bolt straight at me.

Since this was not my first interaction with adventurers, I was prepared and it bounced off my wards and slammed into the halfling who was about to stab me in the back. The poor man shrieked as he dropped to the floor, his last breaths mingling with the smoke from his burned flesh.

With a sigh I snapped my fingers and four tendrils of lava rose up out from beneath the cauldron and stabbed through the chests of the four Elves. Their voices cried out, then dropped down to one voice as three of them vanished, leaving one dying elf laying on the floor.

The grotesque behemoth threw her axe at me and moved to shield the young man. I caught the axe with one hand and caused it to shatter. I then reached out with my power and removed the magical modifications from her twisted body. As she fell to the ground writhing in pain she slowly transformed into a small hunchbacked young woman who looked at the young man with a mixture of love and heartbreak before clutching her actual heart and going still.

Lastly the young man raised his sword and shouted, "For the Great and the Good!"

The sword shot a beam of pure light at me that wasn't strong enough to actually touch my skin. I silently slid forward and put my finger on his crown shaped birthmark. I released my power into his body and felt his own magic resist for a moment before shattering, thus preventing his clean death. He dropped to the ground and lay staring at me, tears welling up in his eyes.

"Hush, child." I said gently, sitting next to him. "You did beautifully. You should be very proud. Best adventurers yet. But you never stood a chance. It is their fault, they should just challenge me directly instead of sending children. Now just go to sleep, you've earned your rest."

After a moment his tears stopped along with his heart, and after shedding some tears of my own, I stood up, signaled for the cleaning crew to come give these heroes a proper burial, and returned to my unending work.

About the Author

Is he a devoted albeit incredibly nerdy father? Is he a Dungeon Master with a penchant for puns? Does he inexplicably have a sizable collection of swords? Has he spent his entire life looking for a way to take the stories that his brain tells him whenever he closes his eyes and convey them to the rest of the world? Is he secretly Superman? The world may never know.

Adult Published Finalist

Tree Rings
Bailey Burke

Delaney slipped her feet, dressed in avocado-patterned socks, into her rollerblades, her hands knowing the motions well. The front wheels were starting to fall apart, becoming half-circles, victims of the concrete of a too-short driveway. Delaney went around in circles every day, counterclockwise, with her thoughts and daydreams.

The mid-April air was crisp. She zipped up her light blue spring jacket, the sleeves a little too short for her now. She adjusted her helmet and set off, one foot in front of the other like her father had taught her years ago.

As Delaney made her rounds, auburn hair sailing behind her turn after turn, a truck pulled up next door. Delaney paused to watch as two men got out, wielding chainsaws. Her heart began to pound. This can't be happening, she thought to herself, biting her lip in nine-year-old dismay.

"Does it have to go?" she called to the men, their orange vests obnoxiously bright against the muted tones of early spring.

"Doesn't stand a chance. Sorry, sweetheart" one of the men called back, his eyes kind but his voice raspy, like the voice of a smoker after days without water.

Delaney sat down on her little front porch to watch the men get started. It was such a shame. The crabapple tree was unusually large, and some of its branches were already crowned in the buds that would turn into stunning pink flowers.

Henry and Delaney would throw the pink petals around like confetti as spring neared its end each year.

"Flower petals are confetti to fairies," Henry had told her.

"Let's both be fairies then," Delaney responded, running to her room to retrieve two pairs of plastic wings. Even though Delaney thought that boys couldn't be fairies, Henry wasn't a boy. Not really. He was Henry. So they danced around the crabapple tree, throwing its fallen petals in the air and chanting to the wizards that lived underground.

Delaney got up from the porch and resumed her routine around the driveway, slower this time, watching as the tree service men began cutting the outermost branches.

Last summer Henry had dared her to climb to the very top of the crabapple tree. She knew the branches couldn't hold her weight, but she went anyway. She never said no to a dare, especially one from Henry. They had an unwritten code.

"Careful, Delaney," Henry had called from his driveway, concern riddling his voice. He was seat-bound at that point already, and Delaney could tell he regretted his dare. But she had a point to prove. She waved triumphantly when she reached the tippy-top, the thin branches swaying under her, like telephone wires under the weight of a flock of birds. But her triumph lasted only a moment. It really wasn't a long fall—it was a crabapple tree afterall, albeit an abnormally large one—but Delaney was shorter then and the fall felt long. She landed funny, and a cracking noise scared her more than the sudden pain in her arm. Henry tried to stand up, but immediately fell back down.

Delaney laughed at the memory. She had been mad at Henry for nearly a full day after that incident. Breaking her wrist meant no rollerblading for nearly a month. She would give anything to be mad at Henry again.

The outermost branches of the almost-blooming tree littered the ground. The vested men paused to scoop them up, dragging them to the back of the truck. Delaney stopped and stared.

The tree looked so naked now. With its outside covering gone, Delaney could see the damage better. Its trunk was split in two, darkened to ash. That explained why the tree was leaning so much to one side—it looked as if it were kneeling towards Delaney's driveway, a peasant bowing to a queen. Delaney had slept through last night's thunderstorm, waking up to soggy grass and branches clumped about the yard every which way. The heart of her and Henry's tree had been zapped to nothingness.

Delaney resumed her laps, feeling the brisk April air on her knee. Nearly every pair of pants she owned had a hole in at least one of the knees, a consequence of years of refusing to wear knee pads. She had grown so much that winter that she would need new pants soon anyway, so her mother had stopped complaining.

One time Delaney ripped a pair of her pants in half. She was playing pirates with Henry, and the crabapple tree was their ship. Her pink velvet pants got caught on a branch as she jumped down, pretending to be pushed overboard by the cruel captain. Henry had laughed and laughed because the rip was right in the center of her butt and he could see her Snoopy underwear.

Delaney had laughed too, because it was just Henry.

The big branches were now gone. Heavy enough where both men carried each one to the truck, thrusting them inside with grunts and muted conversation. The sun was getting lower in the sky, and the vested men were trying to pick up the pace. Delaney knew her mom would be getting up from her nap soon, putting on the news and starting dinner. But Delaney didn't want to go inside until she had said a proper goodbye to the tree. She had to watch it really leave.

Where do trees go when they die? she wondered. Is there a tree Heaven, a forest in the sky where fairies throw around petal confetti and children dance from branch to branch? Henry would know.

Delaney's ankles hurt. She had sped up without realizing it, doing loop after loop at top speed. She stopped and walked over to the grass, her steps awkward and exaggerated in her blades. She sat down, legs criss-crossed, even though it meant her butt got wet. She wanted to watch. Numbly, her fingers clutched the grass. She ripped up pieces and twirled them between her fingers, the fingers that had lost their pudginess and begun to grow long and slender.

When they were six, Henry had taken her hand and haphazardly shoved a ring made out of a fuzzy purple pipe cleaner onto her middle finger.

"The ring means I'm going to marry you one day. My dad told me all about how rings work." Henry had informed her.

"Aren't we too young to be married?" Delaney had asked.

"Right now, yeah. You gotta be at least 10 to be married. But I'm willing to wait."

At the time, Delaney wasn't sure that she wanted to marry Henry. But now she wished she had kept the pipe cleaner ring. She watched as the vested men got closer and closer to the base of the trunk with their chainsaws.

It was a hot, sunny August day when Henry and Delaney had sat at the base of the crabapple tree, their backs against its sturdy and knotted trunk. They could feel its uneven bark and were grateful for its shade. Delaney was dressed all in black, with her Sunday shoes shoved on her seven-year-old feet.

"Do you believe in God?" she had asked Henry.

"Sure." Henry had replied, rolling a fallen crabapple along the ground with his soft hand. "Do you believe in ghosts?" she then asked.

"Yeah. I've seen one before." Henry said matter-of-factly. Delaney nodded in recognition. She remembered the story.

"I wonder if my grandpa's a ghost now."

"Probably not. You have to be a pirate or something dangerous to become a ghost." Henry threw the crabapple into the road.

Delaney could almost feel Henry sneaking up behind her as she watched their tree disappear piece by piece. He always used to try to scare her, poking her in the back of the neck and screaming "Boo!" before dissolving into a fit of laughter. The sun was setting faster now it seemed. She could see the kitchen light on inside her home. Henry's yard looked naked without the branches of the tree shading the grass. Where would the fairies get their confetti now?

Delaney wondered. She brushed herself off and began rollerblading again.

The men were almost done. They used a special tool to dig the bottom of the stump out of the ground. It was louder than the chainsaws, which had become a comfortable background noise. She watched as a maze of roots emerged from below the surface. Henry would tell her that the roots were telephone wires for the wizards that lived underground.

"Every tree has a wizard that lives underneath it," Henry had told her once, as they threw crabapples back and forth over their tree. Henry stopped and scooped up more crabapples and began juggling. He was really good at juggling. He was supposed to teach Delaney last summer.

Delaney wondered if the wizard under their tree had wept with them that fateful January day. Henry had called her on walkie-talkie, his voice breaking and hard to understand over the little speaker. They had embraced in the snow under their tree. Henry was sobbing; it was only the second time that Delaney had seen him cry, and the first time she had heard the word that sounded so foreign in Henry's high-pitched voice. Later that night her mother had explained what 'leukemia' meant.

The men loaded the stump into their truck. Nothing but barren ground remained, the grass matted and torn from the men's work. How would the wizard live without his tree? Mr. Bennett would probably plant grass seed soon, covering up the tree-trunk-shaped bareness that now enveloped the middle of his yard.

It didn't seem fair to Delaney that she should lose two friends in less than a year. There wasn't even a stump left behind for tea parties. Though perhaps Delaney was getting too old for tea parties. The men in their orange vests closed up the back of the truck and got in. Starting the engine, they pulled out of Henry's driveway and left the neighborhood.

"Goodbye, Henry," Delaney whispered. She stood, watching, until the truck disappeared from sight. Then, sighing, she decided to do one last loop around her driveway. Dinner would be ready soon, and Dad would come home.

Gaining speed, she sailed around the curve. As she closed her eyes, she felt the breeze on her rosy cheeks, turned red by the chillness of April. She heard a loud popping sound, and seconds later she was on the concrete, the other knee of her pants ripping in the process. One of her front wheels had cracked and broken, its screw and bits of rubber scattering about the driveway. Her hands had caught her fall, getting scraped by the jagged concrete. She brushed the dirt out of her shallow wounds, knowing that the little pinpoints of blood would disappear in a matter of minutes. It was time for a new pair of skates.

She took off her blades at the end of the driveway and walked to the front door in her avocado-stockinged feet. She paused at the porch and took one last look at the Bennett's empty yard. She felt her eyes welling but she bit the inside of her cheek.

"Promise me you won't cry and be all sad when I'm gone, okay?" Henry had whispered one windy night when he was still well enough for sleepovers in sleeping bags in his carpeted basement.

"I promise." Delaney had even committed to involving her pinky in the matter.

"You'll have to marry someone else," Henry told her, his brown eyes shining in the dark. "Never." Delaney had said, but she didn't promise. They laid in silence, watching as the branches of their crabapple tree danced in the wind outside the little basement window until they drifted off to sleep.

About the Author

Bailey is a sophomore at the University of Michigan studying Creative Writing & Literature and History. In her free time, she leads a letter writing club, is involved in campus ministry, tutors Spanish, and enjoys rollerblading. In the summer, Bailey enjoys tending her garden in Grand Rapids and working at a local greenhouse. She hopes to be a professor and/or published author someday.

Adult Published Finalist

Dance With Me
EF Coigne

Nothing here was a surprise. I had checked it all out on the street level view on my computer.

Narrow houses, each sporting a different color and a mishmash of uniquely unthemed architectural ideas, huddled together shoulder to shoulder as if for protection against being noticed and singled out for demolition. That's what would have happened in my hometown. Try to build something so visually distinct there and you would be asked to tear it down, please, lest it propagate. But this was San Francisco, not Fort Wayne, and the collective effect of the disjointed individual statements was one of complete charm. I was going to love it here.

I parked the silver KIA rental outside my destination, a red brick three-story building with a bakery on the bottom and apartments above. I took in a deep breath of the cool, sunny California morning and climbed halfway up the walled-in stairs, freshly painted bright blue. Then I stopped. It couldn't hurt to bring a gift, a small token. I walked back down the steps and entered the bakery.

I waited in line, savoring the warm aromas. When my turn came I asked the older gentleman behind the counter what Ms Song upstairs liked. He smiled and bagged the last two onion bagels, waving off my attempts to pay.

A woman about my mother's age answered my knock at the third-level door. Black sweatpants and a plain maroon tee. Long graying hair, slender, barefoot, slightly weary face. And not expecting company. She started to close the door, then recognized me.

"Roger? What are you doing here? I told you I would let you know."

"I thought a personal visit would help. You can only do so much on a computer."

"Let me guess. Your father's idea, right?" She held back a small gray kitty with her cane. "Well, you're here. Might as well come in. Don't let Penumbra out. But I'm still interviewing others, you understand."

I entered the renowned Pamela Song Dance Studio, a large empty space under clerestory windows and skylights, one wall covered with mirrors. A living area, just a tiny kitchen and two closed doors occupied maybe one-fourth of the top floor. Pamela gestured for me to sit at the oak table by the large window which overlooked a little park across the street. She raised a coffee cup with an expectant look. I nodded, seated myself and set down the white bakery bag. As she tended to her hospitality I tried to ignore her cane, the symbol of a legendary dancer's career cut short.

She set a steaming mug before me and sat at the adjoining side. She noticed the bag. "Oh.

From Mr Yam. We go way back."

I selected a packet of sweetener from a square wicker basket. "He wouldn't take any money. And yeah, my dad's in sales so to him the face-to-face meeting is everything. Sometimes old men are right, you know?"

"Is he proud of you for wanting to be a personal assistant to a dance instructor? Didn't he want you to be an astronaut or a shark wrestler or something like that?"

The cat jumped up onto my lap. "He's fine. It's my mom that worries. But not about that. She doesn't trust California. She says I won't get the job, and then I'll die in an earthquake."

Pamela sighed. "Well, we might as well get this over with. Your résumé was certainly less than impressive. Under 'accomplishments or recognition in the field of dance, you put 'convincing Susie Williams to go with me to the Senior Prom.'"

"Just a joke. I was trying to stand out, to be remembered. I did include a video and list my production work."

Pamela took a bagel from the sack. "I have to be honest with you, Roger. That was all minor league stuff. And it was pretty straightforward. You lack imagination, a sense of fantasy and... romance, I guess. As for your dancing, I have no doubt you can toss female partners around like so much confetti, but having one dancer noticeably taller and bulkier than the rest is a distraction. Your solos were good, but not outstanding."

"But I have ideas for choreography and staging. I only need a chance."

"You don't just walk into Yankee Stadium and pick up a bat. You have to earn your way there. And here. I'm sorry, Roger."

Outside, a young woman blessed with a dancer's body locked her bicycle to a rack. She shouldered a gym bag and crossed the street to the bakery stairs, a member of the troupe ready to punch the clock. Time for me to go. I cradled the purring cat in my arms, rose from the table and walked to the studio where I would never work, just to stand there one time in the soft light with my dream.

Suddenly, the whole world shook and rumbled. The floor shifted under my feet. Penumbra yowled and clawed her way off me as I stumbled and fell. The dance floor dropped a whole story. Parts of the ceiling collapsed.

The shaking continued for several seconds. When it stopped, I stood and checked myself for damage. I had been lucky. Nothing very heavy had struck me. I clambered over the wreckage of steel and wood and broken glass toward where the kitchen had been. It was now even lower than the studio and the outer wall had fallen into it. I couldn't see Pamela through the whirling dust. I called out. After the third time she answered.

"I'm okay," she cried. "I'm covered in bricks, but I think I can get out if you help me."

I pushed and pulled at the debris blocking my path to her with little effect. "I'll see if I can get some help," I told her. No sooner had those words died than a second shock struck, knocking me down again. A large roof timber fell heavily across my knees. The tremor quieted, the dust settled. I lay there looking up at a patch of beautiful blue sky as the streets screamed with sirens and car alarms.

"Pamela?" No answer. "PAMELA?"

A moan, then a weak voice. "I can't move."

Another tremble tightened the beam's lock on my legs. I asked, "Can you reach your phone?" "It was on the table. Can't see it. Yours?"

"I left it in the car." My father's advice again. "But I'm trapped now."

We were silent for a few minutes, then Pamela said, "They won't get to us in time, will they? They won't bother searching a neighborhood bakery when there are schools and hospitals and big buildings that fell down."

And fires. Wisps of black smoke began to pollute my sky.

A cough. "I can't breathe," Pamela said quietly. "I'm going to die."

I shouted for help, again and again. "I'm scared, too," I confessed. "We should talk. To pass the time."

"Talk? About what? What matters now?" "I don't know. Is the job interview over?" "The job? What's the use?"

"We have to talk about something." I called out to the street again. "What do you ask finalists, the people that have made it past 'I'm sorry?'"

Pamela produced another cough, faint and shallow. "Well... here's one thing I like to ask.

Imagine you... you have a time machine. You can use it three times. Only one rule... You can't change history. You can't go back and... have another shot at an old flame or... or shoot Hitler. So where do you go?"

The hard edge of something pressed against my back. I tried in vain to shift my position. "I guess I'd like to see the most spectacular thing I can imagine. I want to see the formation of the Moon."

"What does that mean?"

"My roommate at Purdue studied astronomy. They think the Moon formed when another planet struck Earth and knocked a bunch of the crust into space. Some fell back down, but most of it came together to make the Moon. That had to be something to see. I'm assuming I'll be safe from harm in a bubble out in space, so I can just relax and watch it all unfold."

"Yes," said Pamela. "Nothing can harm you. What else?"

"There's such a list already. Okay. Still with the heavens, I'd like to bring Galileo to our time and let him look through a modern telescope. Imagine the look on his face. How cool would that be?"

"Those are good answers." Pamela's voice became strained. "Most people don't get it... they want to profit in some way. They say they... want to go back and buy Microsoft cheap, or... write the Beatles' songs before they do... One person had no more imagination than... than wanting to go to Woodstock. So what's... what's your third wish? Do you want to see Nureyev or... or dance with Pavlova?"

I couldn't feel my lower legs. I wondered if I would lose them. For my third wish I was going to say 'go to Woodstock,' but now I answered, "Yes. I want to dance. But with you."

"Me?"

"You. You join me in the time bubble and we fly back to, say, the nineteenth century. We'll go to Paris."

"I don't think I can..."

"You've waited for this all your life. You're sixteen, and you're being introduced to society at a grand ball. I'm a dashing cavalry officer on my way to the Prussian War, and the fourth greatest swordsman in all of France. Dance with me. Please."

Silence. Then, "Only the fourth?"

"Well, that's still very good, and since you're only the sixth most beautiful girl in Paris, I don't think you're in any position to judge."

"Sixth is still kind of pretty, isn't it?"

"In Paris, it's heartbreakingly perfect. You're dressed in a lacy pink full-length gown. Every man there is competing for your attention, but our eyes meet from across the room and you accept my hand for the first waltz."

"I've always loved the waltz," Pamela admitted. "And my dress isn't quite... to the floor. I'm showing a little... white-stockinged ankle, which is even more shocking than my... my rather daring decolletage."

"Yes. Damn the scandal. Don't hide anything. We take the floor with your eyes reflecting the glow of a thousand candles. The orchestra strikes up Strauss. No... Someone less oompah and more passionate. Tchaikovsky. Waltz of the Flowers. It won't be composed for another twenty years but we need it now, because we must soar."

"Yes. Let's soar. We spin madly about the room... without a single wrong step, as if we've... we've danced with each other... since time began."

"It ends too quickly. We run, giddy and breathless, through the tall, open doorway to the cool marble balcony-"

Pamela interrupted. "Where your Moon... your mysterious Moon... has been waiting patiently... for a billion years... for this moment, for you... for you to give me my first kiss."

"One of your suitors, Lieutenant LeMerde, sees that kiss and dares to question your virtue. At dawn, my rapier teaches the swine a sharp lesson about manners."

"That LeMerde was a poor excuse for a... a gentleman. Thank you, sir, for defending... my honor. I am forever in your debt."

"After the duel I rush to the front lines, where I am shot from my mount and die thinking only of your innocent kiss."

"Maybe we could work on that part." Pamela's voice was barely audible over the sounds of a bleeding city.

"Maybe we could." The sky was dark with smoke now, and I could smell gas. I hoped the ovens in the bakery downstairs weren't still glowing. "So do I get the job?" I asked.

The faintest of laughs. "If you still want it."

Mom was wrong. "Thank you," I replied.

I felt the whump of a light explosion beneath us. That dislodged the cat from her hiding place.

She scampered away over the rubble, ahead of billows of eye-stinging smoke. Now our only hope was for that to smother us before the flames arrived.

"Roger?"

"Yes?"

"Dance with me once more... Take me to the prom."

I closed my eyes. "Nineteen sixty-two. A small-town high school gym. We have to take our shoes off. A scratchy Connie Francis 45 plays over a tinny public address system."

Pamela coughed. "Yes. A slow dance. We just... gently sway back and forth... and hold each other tight... until it ends."

About the Author

Grand Rapids born and raised. His mother was a schoolteacher. She gave her children short, simple names so they would be easy to spell. Thus began a life of low expectations. There's room for another sentence? Okay.

This is something the author does not like to flash around lest he appear immodest, but he is licensed by the state of Michigan to operate a motor vehicle on public roads. Honest. Keeping with the regional theme, his main claim to fame is that his wife's mother was a nurse employed by Gerald Ford's proctologist. He (the author, not #38) also picks the bamboo shoots out of his chop suey, believing one should never eat anything better suited for fishing poles.

Adult Published Finalist

Strawberry Jam
Ariella Hillary

It's my first time coming to see you since I left for college. I try to push away that hurt look on your face as I had rushed to leave that sits in the back of my memory. Though looking forward to seeing you, I'm feeling anxious as well. I'm really not sure how this is going to go. My arms are full as I walk across the grass, the ground a little uneven. The trees that dot the way cast shadows with their vast canopies. You would call them romantic. I spot you a little way in the distance, waiting.

"Happy first batch day, sis," I say when I reach you. I'm going for cheerful, but I can hear the trepidation in my voice. I lay out the picnic blanket before you, preparing for what used to be our annual first batch luncheon. The blanket found its way into one of my boxes when I moved out of mom and dad's last year. I run my fingers over the fraying seams holding the patches together. Flowers and Polk-a-dots from old dresses and blankets map our progression through early childhood. Lying down beneath the sun, the worn fabric feeling soft against my skin, I breathe in the old adventures. I glance over at you waiting patiently for me to finish my trip down memory lane. With a relinquishing sigh, I sit back up and reach for the picnic basket. Butter, freshly sliced bread, and this year's first batch of strawberry jam are lined up, eager to be tasted.

I finger the wicker on the side of the basket, remembering when you first got it. It was the only thing you had especially wanted for Christmas that year. You wanted to have picnics in the park like they did in the movies. Mom and dad took me to the store with my allowance money and were patient with me while I picked out the most romantic looking basket. I thought the color of the wicker matched your hair so nicely. There was so much snow outside, but you were so excited to use your new picnic basket that you insisted on us making lunch and having a picnic right there in the living room. I remember you had let me help you make the sandwiches. Our feet dangled from stools as you spread peanut butter on slices of bread and I got to do the jam. We pressed the slices together and then handed them off to mom to wrap in beeswax wraps before placing them in the basket. Dad even made hot chocolate and put it in a thermos for us.

I begin to spread butter on the bread slices, a thin layer on mine and an obscenely thick layer on yours; just as you like it. "Might as well eat it off the spoon," I mumble at you with a smirk, as I have done so many times before. Catching the edge of the lid of the mason jar with my fingernails, I feel the slight pull against my nailbeds as it resists. The sweet hiss of success breaks the quiet as the seal releases. A smooth, ruby surface peeks out from beneath the lid. I pierce through it with the knife, bringing my face close to breathe in the freshly released aromas of sweet, succulent summer. Enticing chamomile is carried in the warm embrace of luscious strawberries. It's strong enough to taste the plump berries that we would sneak bites of as we followed mom down the rows of the strawberry field, juice dripping down our chins and staining our clothes if we accidentally wore too light a color. After mom cleaned and hulled the berries, she would hand them to us in bowls for the next step. Their juices would squelch between our fingers as we crushed their portly bodies. I pretended to be a doctor playing with a bowlful of guts. Eventually, I realized I'd make for a pretty poor doctor if there were guts for me to play with. You refused to let my antics distract you from perfecting the recipes for the bakery you insisted we would someday own. Every year you spouted off bakery name ideas while we picnicked in the park, scarfing down our first batch slices, and every year they'd get more and more ridiculous. But you always came back to the same one.

I spread the jam over the butter. After handing you yours, I take a big bite of mine. The crust crunches as my teeth sink into the tender flesh. Creamy butter intermingles with ripe berries on my tongue. I release a sigh of pleasure as my senses are completely enveloped. My eyes flutter open bringing me back to Earth, our picnic blanket, and your strawberry jam laden bread resting on top of your headstone, untouched. I crawl over, closing the distance between myself and the stone, and trace over the inscription. Beloved daughter and sister. The sharp edges are beginning to soften from the elements. I take another bite of my bread. There's a twinge in the back of my jaw from the tang of the jam. The surface of the stone is smooth and hard as I lean my forehead against it, but the sun has made it warm. I swallow the mouthful and exhale the breath I was holding with it.

"Remember when you used to force feed me all of your baking?" On the weekends, in the height of your mania, you would have so many different versions of the same thing while testing out the different recipes. They would all be shoved in my face for me to distinguish between the varied nuances. Cookies and breads and muffins and scones. There was no end to it, only for you to create another stack of recipes for the following weekend. Every Friday, when we got home from school, I would barricade myself in my room to avoid the onslaught of sugar coma. I had never conceived that before I even graduated high school, I would be avoiding the kitchen for a different reason altogether.

You had just graduated, your life just getting ready to go. The cancer changed everything so fast. We all watched as you kept on baking and creating, even as you wasted away. Mom and dad were so strong. They took you to your appointments and sat with you in the kitchen listening as you regaled them with your ideas. I continued to hole up in my room like a coward, burying myself in school work. What bothered me most was your eyes. They had lost their shine except for the faint gleam that would fill them when you brought a new side-by-side of cookies or lemon curd for me to compare. Every time you tapped on my door, I had to fight harder and harder to hide how much I hated you for making me look at you. Your once golden waves, the color of your picnic basket, now limp and brassy. I'd swallow a bite of each of your offerings before pointing to the one I liked best. You smiled at my participation and whisked away to the kitchen, while I shut the door again and returned to trying to numb myself with schoolwork.

Graduation finally came, followed by an unabating summer. My suitcases were packed to bursting two weeks before I left for college. I hardly embraced you to say good-bye. The basket of muffins you sent with me all went to my roommate and her friends. I didn't touch a single one. While I was away, I could forget. During holidays, I stayed with friends, voicing a curiosity to see other parts of the country. Forgetting began to come easily, until mom and dad called to tell me your days were numbered. I hung up without even saying anything and went right back to studying to try harder to forget again. There were too many distractions. I needed all my mental capacity if I were to even hope to pass my MCAT and get into medical school. They messaged me the funeral arrangements when I didn't pick up my phone three days later. And I kept studying.

I stayed for summer classes. My brain was completely saturated with covalent bonds and human anatomy when I received a package from mom. She had sent me a jar of strawberry jam. I threw it in the garbage. Almost immediately, I pulled it back out and set it on the edge of the desk. It was an easy push back into the bin if I decided to. I stared at the little seeds through the glass. I could almost taste the sweet summer memories as I imagined crunching them between my teeth like I did as a little girl. When I got home from classes that night, I pulled a spoon I had taken from the dining hall out of my jacket pocket. I lost my resolve, pried the lid open, and plunged the spoon inside. Having not had sweets in so long, it was almost cloying. I savored that first bite, letting the jam melt in my mouth until the seeds were all that was solid. My tongue moved as if on autopilot, pressing them against the roof of my mouth before pushing them between my teeth for that familiar crunch. I hadn't felt the tears come. The next morning, I found myself in my bed still in yesterday's clothes, my pillow damp and cold against my cheek. I packed all my things and went back home.

I awake from my reverie, my back against your headstone. "Turns out my path to becoming a doctor really was doomed," I say. "I guess I enjoyed the squishing too much." But I know the truth is my heart wasn't in it. I think a part of me felt I could somehow bring you back through healing others and be able to make up for all the time had I lost. In that one spoonful of jam, I realized that the way back to us was through our joy.

When I returned home, it was another month before I was able to brave your bedroom and find your baking journal. With mom's help, I immediately got to work. I put on your apron and stepped into the kitchen for the first time in forever. I turned on the oven for the first time in even longer. I set your journal on the counter and opened it to the first recipe. You were always so meticulous; everything was easy to follow. And you had trained my tastebuds so well. Mom sat on the other side of the island, sometimes with dad. They recounted your ideas, and we felt your presence. Through the course of a year, I perfected every one of your recipes. I was even courageous enough to add a couple new ideas to the mix.

I finish my bread, sucking the jam and butter off my fingertips. The sun feels so warm on my face as I rest my head against the stone a little longer. With one last deep breath, I open my eyes and come away from the stone. Across the way, I notice a freshly dug grave and some people in varying shades of black starting to gather behind it. Flowers dotted many graves in between; some fresh, some almost forgotten. A couple flags dotted graves here and there, and some trinkets on others. Many were empty. I know mom and dad wouldn't have left yours empty and bleak, but I think about how long it took me to get here and I'm sorry for it. I begin to collect all the picnic items to put back in the basket. After putting the lid back on the jam jar, I wipe the sticky drip off the Two Sisters' Bakery label. My hand hesitates as I'm about to place the jar in the picnic basket. I think better of it and decide to set it next to your slice of bread instead. I press my fingers to my lips, then back to your stone before heading back to the bakery.

About the Author

Ariella moved to Michigan's beautiful Upper Peninsula with her mother and sisters as a little girl. She spent her childhood on the shores of Lake Superior before venturing cross country upon joining the military. The trees and Superior shoreline called her home, where she now resides with her husband, son, two dogs, and a cat. When she's not working, she's with her family enjoying nature, books, movies, and bubble baths.

Teen Judges' Choice Winner

Multitudes of Blue
Lani Khuu

The mid-August air hums with an electric mugginess. It is charged with monotony, and I feel like I am drowning in layers and layers of television static. The numbing sensation begins at the tip of my nose and drips down my throat and into my lungs. Once it gets into my lungs, there's not much I can do. It tickles the base of my throat and tiptoes between my ribs, expanding, insistent on taking up air and space. My body is an involuntary beehive, constantly pestered by a covert melody, a vast emptiness seeping out of me like sweet, sweet honey. It hums with stingers poised and at the ready as it continues to claim my body as its own. It paints blue stripes behind my eyelids. I'm not sure I will ever find out where it comes from. Caroline sometimes said that she felt strange, that the cavernous expanse inside her chest was beginning to flood. I wonder if she could ever find the drain.

Beside me, Parker takes a gulp from a glass bottle which he smuggles out of his sweatshirt sleeve and passes over. He looks like he is melting into his swing seat like a wax candle, sweat dripping down the jagged crook of his nose, mingling between his spattered freckles. Mama used to take Caroline and I to this playground sometimes.

I take the bottle from him and droplets of condensation run off the bottle and between my fingers. My cracked fingertips sting as the dampness cuts through dry, papery skin. I hoist the bottle to my lips and take a swig. It is bitter, warm, and flat. Underwhelming. I hold the liquid in my mouth for a moment and push it through my teeth, letting bubbles form and run down the raw pink of my gums. I think it might be beer, but I am not sure because I am only sixteen today. I consider spitting it out, but Parker gives me a look which makes me think that sixteen is practically a woman.

I remember the day that Mama got married. Caroline and I were three. We wore matching tulle skirts, and Mama spent hours weaving her delicate fingers through Caroline's hair. Caroline had the same blonde curls that Mama does, the ones that she used to iron because Jonathan said she looked beautiful that way. The same blonde curls that always seemed to bounce when she walked; the ones that were never dull and seemed to glow when the sun was setting. She spent hours taming Caroline's hair before pulling mine into a simple plait. When Grandma wasn't talking about how it was only right that Jonathan would marry mama after we were born, she was talking about how I looked just like him. She said that Caroline was Mama's twin, that I was Jonathan's. To Caroline, he was Papa, the man who read her bedtime stories. To Grandma, he was the scoundrel that robbed her daughter of a future, that plucked her unripe potential and crushed it beneath his heel. He was the reason that Grandma had to stop being a mother. The reason her daughter would have half a childhood before she was forced to provide one for the two baby girls entwined beneath the flesh of her swollen belly. She had only been sixteen. I'm not sure what he was to Mama when they got married. By that time, she was nineteen and peeled her wedding dress from her body like a scab the moment the reception had ended. Maybe he was just the scar tissue.

Parker has been watching me. He has finished off the bottle and he's looking at me expectantly. His eyelids droop and his voice picks up as he asks if I want to get out of here. I plant my feet into the wood chips and grimace when the swing seat tugs at my skin. I feel as if I am floating and someone has filled my ears with quicksand. My skin is too tight for my body, it's just another thing in this town that I've outgrown. It stings, the sensation of skin pulling away from bone. I am afraid to blister, so I bite my tongue and swallow all of Grandma's warnings about boys with cigarettes clenched between their teeth. Her warnings taste of cherry cough syrup and sugar cubes. The aftertaste lingers, sickening and sticky, on my bottom lip when I tell him yes. Yes, I want to get out of here.

I leave my bike in front of a street lamp, not bothering to chain it, and get into the passenger seat of Parker's cherry red pickup truck. He clicks on the radio and turns it up so that we can feel Kurt Cobain's five-packs-a-day growl vibrating beneath the seats. A lonely guitar riff sits on top of the suffocating, small town air, and it thickens. It thickens just enough so that it is as opaque and heavy as wet cement when I pull it into my lungs. It collides with the buzzing, the humming, between my ribs, but does not push it out. They dance around each other in a skittery cadence. It is all feathery light touches and chalkboard nails. The numbing sensation wraps around my skull, encasing it like plaster. I don't even notice when Parker lights a cigarette, clenches it between his teeth, and throws his arm around me.

Jonathan used to read us bedtime stories. Caroline always listened. She propped her head up against a pillow, getting drunk off sugar coated whispers. I could never listen. Instead, I searched for constellations in the swirled stucco ceiling. I tried so desperately to hold onto the part of myself that believed in bedtime stories, the part that could choke on the sweet lace of childhood. The part of myself that didn't hear Mama screaming at Jonathan when she thought we were asleep. By middle school, Caroline and I knew that we were a mistake. That our existence, that the living and breathing, the filling of our soft pink lungs, the pumping of silvery blood to our premature hearts was never supposed to happen. That we were the record stopping in the midst of Mama's adolescence. We knew she wanted to rewind it, to tell her sixteen year old self that it wasn't love and she was still a child. If I knew how, I would rewind it for her time and time again.

Caroline cried a lot. When she thought I was fast asleep across the room, she wept for Jonathan. Jonathan, our father, who lost Mama in the blight of her own self pity. Jonathan, who thought that stained glass and wedding bands could bring back the blooming teenage girl whose kisses tasted of lemongrass and honeydew. She wept for Grandma, who swaddled Mama in her arms one day and was forced to watch as the world chipped and molded her baby into a woman before she had the chance. But she never wept for Mama. Never for Mama, who was only sixteen. Never for Mama, who traded her childhood for a boy she couldn't even love back.

Parker drives until it is dark. We cling tightly to the backroads where we can listen to music as loudly as we want and drive as fast as we want. There is nobody else around for miles. We roll down the windows and scream his favorite songs at the top of our lungs. I think that if I scream loudly enough, it might wake up that part of me that has grown so accustomed to being numb. It still clings to my insides, that murky, perpetual nothingness.

For a moment, I think that it is late and I should get home to mama. The sun has kissed the horizon line and is long gone. But then I remember Mama's tears on the day that Jonathan left with Caroline in tow. Torn over the absence of half a future she never wanted. Torn over the daughter with a peaked nose and golden curls. The one who held a mirror to Mama's adolescence. The one who left with the only man who ever loved Mama. Some nights, Mama can't look at me. Half the daughter she lost and half the man responsible for the loss. But tonight, I am sixteen and I feel like being looked at.

Parker pulls over and turns off the radio. The silence is loud and foreign, like a native tongue which I have long forgotten. The rounded vowels sound like home, yet I can't quite seem to bring them together. He reaches into the backseat and produces a bottle of wine.

"For the birthday girl," the words hang off his lips like a dare.

He uncorks the bottle with a sharp pop which cuts through the chalky silence. He doesn't have cups, so we pass the bottle between us, taking turns pulling warm sips of strawberry scented euphoria from the glass rim in silence until the bottle is empty and the dead august heat becomes perfumed and balmy. He tosses the empty bottles out of his open window and I flinch as it shatters against the hard packed dirt. Parker looks at me with raised brows and lets out a laugh which slithers down the column of my spine and sits cold and dead in the pit of my stomach. I cling to discomfort because it is better than feeling empty.

His words are slurred and my senses are waterlogged. The filmy residue of guilt wrapping around the pillar of my throat nearly escapes me as I think of Mama pacing around the dinner table. Parker turns the music back on. For a moment, he just sits with his hands pressed to his temples, the same way Jonathan did when he got home from work. Then, he places them on the steering wheel and grips it so tightly that his knuckles are bone white, and I remember that Jonathan used to do that. Caroline said it was because he was stressed from work. Mama didn't say much at all. Caroline always hated her for the way she hated Jonathan, for the regret that followed her recklessness. I turn on the radio. It cuts in and out of the chorus. I turn it up loud enough that I can feel it resonating in my chest like a second heartbeat, but Parker's stony silence rings so heavily that I can feel it ricochet off my teeth. His silence is deafening. It is the kind of silence that makes itself known. The kind that reminds me that there is nobody else around for miles. The kind that reminds me that I am only sixteen, which makes me feel smaller, almost small enough to fit back into my skin. His rage is a piping scarlet red, so bright that I can see it through the cigarette smoke lingering in the mere feet between our bodies. I think of Caroline hating Mama for sitting motionless at the kitchen table while Jonathan stood nearby, teeth clenched and choking on anger, and I ask Parker if he is alright. I learn why Mama stayed silent as he reaches through the smoke, bridges the space between us, and smears his red hot anger in the hollows of my cheeks.

For a moment, I think that I might be colorblind because right now, anger doesn't feel crimson and fiery. No, it feels delicate and baby blue. Like if I breathed too deeply, it would shatter. His hands are cold, but his lips are scalding as they come crashing into mine. They are shards of glass, and I do not want to get cut. I pull back, dazed and on the verge of regret. I turn off the music because I picture Mama, sixteen and sucking on the hard knot of womanhood. I picture Jonathan carrying buckets and buckets of bitter blue. He has more than he knows what to do with, and Mama has only ever tasted the syrupy violets that little girls do.

I look at Parker and his cheeks are sunken in and his skin is sallow, worn out by the acidity that comes with this sort of affliction, the kind that comes with blue. Right now, he is drowning in a curdled ultramarine and reaches for me like I am a life vest. I know what comes next because it raised me, and I say stop. But the words drip off my tongue like molasses. It does not hold its shape in his mouth.

He turns the music back on. There is nobody around for miles.

When Parker and I get back to the playground, he asks me if I want to load the bike into the truck and offers to bring me home. I say no thank you, but the thing that trails it out of my lungs screams what have you done? I bite down on the words and they shatter between my teeth as Parker drives away.

As I pedal home, I try to ignore the ache running along my legs and snaking up my neck.

I dismiss the sting crawling over my lips like a spidery kiss, because I begin to think that the world is not very forgiving to children who do adult things and go looking for shoes that are much too large for them. The ringing in my ears is accompanied by the ghost of Parker's icy fingertips trailing up my leg and tracing spirals against my papery skin for miles and miles. His frigid touch follows me home, nipping at my heels, and I am carved hollow.

I recall Caroline and I's fifteenth birthday as I near home. It was two days before they left. Two days before she begged me to come with them because Mama could never love us just like she could never love Jonathan. We walked home from the bus stop, and Jonathan was asleep on the couch. Mama was in the kitchen rolling pie dough between her stick figure fingers. The house smelled like nutmeg, and the sun was casting buttery yellows through the kitchen window, illuminating Mama's sharp face in the soft ring of a halo. She looked young, near ethereal, with cinnamon sprinkled across the bridge of her nose and flour dusted lashes. That day, she let Caroline and I roll out sticky handfuls of dough which we later watched rise to a golden peak in the oven. Jonathan remained asleep on the threadbare couch, apple pie masking the scent of gin on his clothes.

When I get home, the house is hushed and my face is damp with saltwater and sin. My footsteps echo, and hits of cinnamon sugar linger in the air. The smell seeps into my skin, and I hope that I will smell that way forever. In the living room, Mama is asleep on the couch. The television casts yellow lighted shadows which dance across the curve of her cheekbones. Her brows are relaxed, and she looks soft around the edges. Caroline never looked like that. No, my sister was all jagged edges and hardened corners. A cold apple pie sits on the second hand coffee table. I snag a fork from the kitchen and sink the metallic prongs into Mama's pie. It is flaky and sweet, melting into my tongue like the times when the house didn't ring so empty that my presence felt like an intrusion. When the bed across the room was filled with Caroline's airy giggles rather than cobwebs.

On the television, a woman in a pencil skirt predicts slight showers for the upcoming week, and Mama stirs in her sleep. The part of me which longs for my sister, the part which yearns to be longed for asks Why couldn't you just love him, Mama? But the part of me that had been with Parker, the boy with cigarettes clenched between his teeth; the part that has seen a multitude of blues, numbing, thrashing, and hurting, knows that she did love him. She loved the parts of Jonathan that he wrapped in blue cloth, the parts that he slathered in sapphire paints.

Mama saw more shades of blue than anyone I'd ever known. She had oceans of it. Of that thing that always rose to the top of my chest and spilled out between my teeth, buoyant and infinite.

We had only been sixteen. Sixteen when blue lipped boys started giving us blue lipped kisses. And for Mama, it had been okay because it was love, it was love, it was love, and that was what you did when you loved somebody. You took their hurt and made it all your own. When they splashed navy paints into their navels, you dotted it beneath your shoulder blades. But when you are sixteen, still a child even though everything inside you screams otherwise, love paints itself in multitudes of blue. Mama didn't know that blue dried so quickly, that she'd be choking on its residue for the rest of her life. She didn't know that it would be bitter and lonely. She didn't know that it would leave stains on her palms and in the valley between her breasts.

When Caroline and I were toddlers, Jonathan could never get us to bed. Mama would hold us in her lap and rock us to sleep. I think a part of me is still there, asleep against Mama's heartbeat while Caroline tries to wake me.

I turn off the television and we are folded into the fabricky darkness. The street lamp on the corner flickers through the window. Mama sits up, wipes the sleep from her eyes, and I begin to cry deep blue tears as the silence hums a lullaby.

She holds me as I curl into her chest, trying to find myself in her ocean of blue, and we both try to remember how it feels to be fifteen.

About the Author

Lani Khuu is a student from Byron Center, Michigan. She is a captain on her school's cheerleading team, a member of the Michigan Youth Climate Strike finance and logistics team, and a member of the March For Our Lives outreach team. Her work has previously been published in Up North Lit. She hopes to study English and political science in the future.

Teen Judges' Choice Runner-Up

Edwin_Memory_Drive: loaded
Abigail Kloha

Initiating memory drive at 10:30 P.M. Eastern Regulation Hours.

Continue with written data.

Glitches buzz through my circuits as Mrs. Xashivan takes another swig from her wine glass and continues berating whoever she's on the phone with. Sovyn, Zamso, and I watch her silently, acting completely unperturbed aside from a few shared glances. We see how she gestures towards the neon cityscape of Oqulix like it's insulted her. We see how she glares at passing hover trams like they're purposefully trying to interrupt her. We see how her voice becomes fuller as the wine bottle empties.

The children should be doing their homework but have been reading the same screens for the past twenty minutes. They feel the tension growing like I do. Though their sense comes from simple self-preservation and mine from analyzing the similarities of incidents in my memory drive, we both know where this is going.

Mrs. Xashivan raises her voice until it cracks. The children jump. My glitches flicker more forcefully against my coding. I stash the error messages away — aside from the occasional boost in my emotional readouts from the children, they only disturb the strict order of my coding.

And now is not the time for such weaknesses.

Sovyn looks up at me. "Edwin?" she breathes, barely moving her lips. "Please do something."

Zamso, the warmth fading from his dark skin, echoes his older sister's plea through his eyes.

"Let's go finish your work in your room," I say. My voice modulator is set to the lowest volume, but Mrs. Xashivan still sends a sharp glare in my direction. That is all though.

I help Sovyn and Zamso gather their textscreens and digital pens into my caretaker unit satchel. My eyes are always on Mrs. Xashivan. She is still arguing and ingesting alcohol, but her attention is completely on whoever she is speaking to. As long as that continues long enough for the children to reach their bedroom, we will have a relatively peaceful night.

I usher Sovyn and Zamso in front of me as we leave the living room. I walk quickly — not fast enough to concern the children, but enough to abate the glitches sprouting from my memory drive. I do not know why it has chosen this moment to load past scenarios of when we were slow in our escapes, but I walk faster regardless.

We're in the entrance hall. At the base of the stairs.

Half-way up the stairs.

A single curse shoots from the living room, followed by the buzz of an ended phone call and an explosion of footsteps we can't get away from fast enough.

Mrs. Xashivan is at the foot of the stairs, her rigid scowl painted turquoise from the stairs' light strips.

"Sovyn. Zamso. What are you doing?"

I shift down a step, and the children slink behind me. They cling to my stiff white uniform with shaking hands. They are silent. I would do anything to take them away from here, to somewhere they can laugh and play and ramble without confrontations like this.

"Are you deaf or just ignoring me?" Mrs. Xashivan rubs her brow. "Edwin, tell me."

I hesitate. There is no telling what answer will or will not upset her. There is no point in considering the matter though. I cannot lie. It is against my coding, which cannot and should not be broken. It is just as well; any lie could be exposed by the simple removal and reading of my memory drive.

"I am taking the children to do homework in their bedroom," I reply. "A focused environment will be optimal for learning. They will not disturb you in the living room or Mr. Xashivan in his office."

My answer was unsatisfactory.

Mrs. Xashivan goes into a flurry. She scolds the children for not having their homework done due to laziness and irresponsibility. That then spirals into how hard they make her life and how they are the cause of complications and arguments in her workplace. I cannot follow her logic. I am uncertain there is any logic.

I focus on Sovyn and Zamso then. They squeeze my hands, and though my coding gives me no reason to do so, I squeeze back. Sovyn's soft, dark features are hardening, the gentleness in her eyes fading into something cold and sharp — a look most thirteen-year-olds are not capable of. Zamso lets his curls tumble over his face, and he shrivels in on himself, tugging on my hand like I can make it all better.

But I can't.

I've never been able to.

Glitches and errors spin through me. I know what's next. We all do.

There's nothing I can do though and no one in Oqulix cares to help. My coding tells me to stay put and act when ordered, so that is what I must do. It cannot be wrong. No matter how much I struggle to suppress the glitches, I must remember that following my coding will always lead to the best outcome. Somehow.

"Sovyn, Zamso, come down here," Mrs. Xashivan says, her rant now finished.

Zamso whimpers. Sovyn locks her jaw. "Edwin, bring them here."

Glitches crash through my every circuit, violent and tingling with foreign numbers and symbols. They lock my limbs, clashing against my coding that says the order must be followed because how can the glitches possibly know better? How can they be correct when their faulty numbers are clearly making me defective?

The glitches do not know better. Something is simply wrong with me, but I must still maintain optimal functionality.

With loose grips on Sovyn and Zamso's hands, I guide them down the stairs. Mrs. Xashivan wrenches their hands from me when I inexplicably struggle to let go. They begin walking back towards the kitchen, and I am ordered to follow. Sovyn thrashes against her mother, Zamso lets out quiet sobs, and I can do nothing. Mrs. Xashivan spouts foul language until they reach the kitchen door, where she pauses long enough to give me an order: stand silent and unmoving by the living room window until I am told otherwise. I do so. I stand across the room from the kitchen door as Sovyn and Zamso stumble through it, hands reaching for me. My memory drive stumbles over that freshly recorded data, replaying the fear in their eyes far more than needed.

Mrs. Xashivan continues yelling at them in the kitchen, her voice cold and sharp even with sound-absorbing walls between us.

My glitches are worse than they've ever been in the few years I've been aware of them.

Usually keeping them smothered in my programs works sufficiently, but that tactic is now failing. The error messages and warning signals won't stop. They swell with renewed force every time Mrs. Xashivan raises her voice. I struggle to think. I cannot let the errors overpower me. I know they are bad. If I let them win, I'm certain they would cause my programs no end of functionality issues — and the children deserve a working caretaker unit, not a broken one.

Through the kitchen walls, I can now hear Sovyn and Zamso arguing back. Compared to Mrs. Xashivan, their voices are small and in need of protection. The glitches spiral, spreading to the bottom of my feet and the tips of my grey fingers, now twitching with the effort of staying still.

My coding must be telling me to remain a bystander for a reason — there has to be another way to help the children, a new plan that requires me to stay here. What is it then? I close my eyes in a vain attempt to ignore the warning messages and focus.

Since direct confrontation is not an option due to my coding, I would have to escape somewhere with the children. Our own resources are finite, so we'd have to find someone to help us within a day. The children's friends and family members are not an option. They refuse to even acknowledge Sovyn and Zamso's situation, lest it end with a confrontation with Mr. and Mrs. Xashivan. The Oqulix Security Division is equally useless since Mr. and Mrs. Xashivan can more than easily buy their innocence regardless of what we say. Perhaps I would be able to persuade others to help us if I had direct evidence of what happens here, but I have none. Such as now, I have always been ordered away when anything happens, and while sobbing and bruises are suspicious they are nothing without direct evidence of the cause.

The facts and the conclusion are the same as always: I cannot help the children as a bystander.

Then if I have no other way to protect the children, why won't my coding let me go to them?

The yelling in the kitchen swells from both the children and Mrs. Xashivan. My lower core processor feels cold and tight as muffled footsteps race around the kitchen. I wait for it to end in a scream or impact, but slow footsteps on the stairs and down the hall is all that follows.

Mr. Xashivan darts into the room, eyes flickering between me and the kitchen door. His dark skin is glistening with sweat as the yelling continues with sporadic rushes of footsteps. He moves to the wine bottle in the living room and takes a deep drink, his back to the door and eyes on Oqulix's nighttime landscape. I do not know if he is considering joining the mess in the kitchen or returning to the safety of his office. What I do know is that the children's situation will only worsen if he is in the kitchen.

I could persuade him to go back to his office. I could help Sovyn and Zamso. But that would require speaking, and I have been ordered into silence.

I lock my jaw. The glitches are threatening to burst from my mouth in the form of words as my coding struggles to smother them under heaps of virus-free software. I cannot talk because I have been ordered to do so, and my coding clearly states following orders is the best and only way to function. I am made to listen to coding. It is easy and logical and doing otherwise would likely disable me, rendering me useless to the children. Every other caretaker unit listens to their coding without issue, so why shouldn't I?

If I and I alone attempt to find fault in my coding when thousands of others use it daily without complaint, then the fault must lie with me and not the coding. I must be the broken one.

But what if the fault is with the coding regardless of the statistics of those who accept it?

What if I'm not the only one grappling with glitches?

Glass shatters in the kitchen, Mr. Xashivan curses, and my glitches redirect their forces to my memory drive. The faulty strands of numbers swarm the drive and elicit highly unnecessary

data of me bandaging some of the children's worst scars. The error messages multiply. Mr. Xashivan's swearing sounds like it's coming from another room now, though he's only a few feet away from me. I barely register the blurred vision of him shooting across the room, entering the kitchen, and slamming the door behind him.

What?

What?

The glitches are hindering my thinking. My sensory receptors are struggling to process. Why did I just allow Mr. Xashivan to go into the kitchen? I knew that it would only make Sovyn and Zamso's situation worse. What would've been wrong with a few gentle words to coax Mr. Xashivan back into his office? It seems harmless. My coding had stopped me though. Why? Where is the logic in that? I am a caretaker and I was trying to care for the children. Why is my coding restricting me? Why does it smother my glitches which are only trying to protect the children? Shouldn't it support any action for the wellbeing of Sovyn and Zamso? Why does it insist the glitches' sense of right and wrong actions is so unorthodox?

Why does my coding insist I am broken for thinking differently from the instructions every other caretaker unit takes without question?

The voices of all the Xashivans rise in a crescendo of shouting and frantic footsteps and crying and pleading, all of it a mess, a terrifying mess. Something slams and I hear Sovyn begging any god or technology to listen to her little voice.

Why is my coding telling me to stay here? Why does it tell me breaking orders is bad? Break?

Bad? Bad?

Why? Why? Why?

I do not care if I am broken and bad. I am going to protect Sovyn and Zamso.

I take a step forward. Then another one, letting the glitches free from their confines. Now I'm walking towards the kitchen door. I have no plan, and with the mess of coding and glitches struggling through me, I have no time to make one.

A vague idea occurs to me as I touch the door's handle.

A quick diagnostic shows my memory drive is at peak operation. Perfect.

I whip open the door and capture a clear view of parents adding to the collection of bruises on their own children, faces clearly displayed for easy identification.

Next, it's all a blur of Mr. and Mrs. Xashivan racing towards me and shoving and hitting and glass crunching and ignoring orders to stop and the children sobbing. Then it's over. I'm on the ground and so are Mr. and Mrs. Xashivan — unconscious for at least an hour due to alcohol and blows to the head. Everything is still.

At least I think so.

My sensory receptors are suffering from the clashing of my coding and glitches more than I had expected — even more so now that both coding and errors are reeling from the physical confrontation and wave of ignored orders. The spasm of numbers blurs Sovyn and Zamso's figures and muffles their steady breathing. Even when I focus, I can only vaguely make out the violet light reflecting off of shattered glass and the children's tear stricken faces. I cannot walk or even stand. Keeping my sensory receptors alert and my memory drive recording is taking enough effort as it is.

Regardless, I manage to crawl the few feet between the children and I. Sovyn mouths my name. Maybe she's actually saying it and my audio processors are fritzing.

"Take my memory drive," I say. I slump against the counter and look at them until their round faces topped by halos of curly hair are in focus. "It now has evidence on it. Use it to get protection, hopefully outside of Oqulix. I will stay here and catch up with you later."

Sovyn and Zamso lean against me and my senses receptors focus. They are injured, and it hurts to watch them flinch from the fresh bruises. "I'm scared," Sovyn murmurs. "We don't want to go without you."

"Fear is a perfectly normal reaction." My voice modulator grates with static, as though the cacophony of glitching and coding is spilling out through my mouth. "You'll be safe soon. I will find you once you've reached someone who will keep you safe."

Sovyn and Zamso glance at one another. "Promise?" they ask.

My coding has maintained enough functionality to tell me I am in no state to move, and a temporary shutdown is imminent. I physically can't follow them. I will shut down here and be destroyed by the Xashivans upon their return to consciousness. That is my coding's scenario with the highest probability.

But I am now in a habit of ignoring my coding, so my chances of survival do not matter. "I promise."

The children hug me and I do my best to hug them back, minding where their skin is turning blue and purple — the last time it will be anything but a gentle brown. They will find help. With the evidence now on my memory drive, they will finally reclaim some semblance of the childhoods they've been deprived of.

I put my hand on the left part of my chest, over the small indent of my memory drive.

Despite the way my senses are breaking and melding with static, there's a release of tension in my circuits as I realize I helped protect the children. That, despite my technological turmoil, I still managed to help them.

And perhaps, despite my technological turmoil, I neither am nor ever have been broken. I press down on my memory drive and it—

Memory drive was removed at 11:07 P.M. Eastern Regulation Hours. To review written data, press replay.

To finish reviewing written data, remove memory drive from Oqulix Middleschool Chip Decoder. If caretaker unit is available for reactivation, place memory drive in designated slot.

Processing.

Processing.

Drive accepted. Initiating reactivation of Edwin, caretaker unit of Sovyn and Zamso Xashivan.

About the Author

Abigail is a junior at St. Johns High School. She works at the Animal Lodge taking care of dogs, but as much as she loves drowning in cute puppies, she plans on attending college and pursuing a degree in publishing or translation. When she's not writing about people, places, and things that don't actually exist, she enjoys playing the piano, kayaking, volunteering, and spending time with friends. She also likes theater and learning languages. She has a puppy named Oliver, a cat named Perry, and three horses named Maverick, Eva, and Maddie, all of whom are the cuddliest creatures when not begging her for food.

Teen Readers' Choice Winner

Remember?

Hannah Haines

I placed the player needle on the record ever so delicately. I couldn't afford to damage it. Ella Sings Gershwin was my absolute favorite album and if scratched, Alfie would insist that it wasn't worth spending our meager pay on a new copy.

Alfie really was the best husband I could possibly receive; when we'd married, all the girls in the neighborhood had been jealous. They'd cried, "Oh, Mary, you must be something special for such a handsome man to espouse you!" I, of course, glowed with pride, all while insisting "Who's to say he's not the one drawn to me!" Ours had been a whirlwind romance, married straight out of high school- we had met during senior year, and my parents' shock at the engagement so soon after had almost driven me away. I worried that I was making a mistake, but Alfie reassured me. Our love could never have been wrong, we belonged together! Three years of marriage and I still believed that wholeheartedly. He'd always done right by me.

Still, Alfie was practical, and didn't believe in spending our small amount of money on silly pleasures like records. Frivolous and useless, Mary, he argued.

But they weren't useless to me. In the middle of winter, a blizzard raging outside, Ms.

Ella Fitzgerald was a breath of new life in our tiny home. With her tunes cleansing every room, I could almost believe that spring had strolled through the front door. Why, Alfie is supposed to be home from work by now, I registered vaguely, but with my music playing, I had not a care in the world. As the sweeping melodies enveloped me, I stood from the upholstered armchair I'd been sitting in.

My eyes flicked to the textured chair suspiciously, not recalling having it installed before. No matter, perhaps I'd simply forgotten about the purchase. I pressed my hands to my heart and closed my eyes, swaying along to the music. The tempo swelled in my chest, as if it had invaded my body, bathing my very soul. Yes, spring is here.

I heard the front door slam, snapping me out of my reverie, and the needle jumped at the vibration it sent along the walls. I frowned and drifted to the player, intending to inspect the record. It didn't appear scratched, but Alfie knew not to slam the door like that! Besides the danger it posed to my records, it was simply impolite.

"Alfie?" I called, with a slight note of irritation. I grimaced at the sound. I didn't mean to be cross, but more pressing was the creaking in my voice. My husband's name had come out more like the vocalization of an old wagon wheel than the soft bells of my normal voice. I cleared my throat. I sounded positively old, but I still had at least another thirty years before that point. Maybe I was coming down with something, a cold perhaps?

"Granny?" A young woman called, presumably in answer to me, but I wasn't expecting anyone besides Alfie from work. As she strolled into view, setting down a purse on my counter, I took a step back, alarmed. She was peculiar looking, wearing tight denim bottoms that rose past her waist and a neon pink sweater. Strange attire. I rarely saw women out of tea dresses, and nothing like this.

"Granny?" She repeated. Her leisurely expression morphed into concern as she turned her gaze on me.

I shook my head. "I'm no one's grandmother. I think you've got the wrong house, dear." I clutched the edge of the table next to me, unnerved by this young girl who'd broken into my home. Who did she think she was? She must have been confused.

I had expected her to leave, but she only moved closer, grabbing my hand, an expression that vaguely resembled desperation contorting her features. "It's me, Granny Mary. Remember? I'm your granddaughter, Lila?"

I jerked away from her grip, and this time she didn't follow me. "I don't know you," I insisted, my wobbly voice growing progressively louder. "We've not met. Please leave. My husband will be home soon and he will not stand for this!" I jutted my chin out, hoping to present a strong stance.

At my words, an inexplicable bout of sadness crossed the girl's face. Her lip quivered, and it appeared as if she might cry. I hadn't the slightest idea why, but I did not have time to inquire about it before it disappeared with her deep inhalation. She nodded a casual goodbye, retreating to the counter and picking up her purse.

"Of course," She responded, slinging the strap over her shoulder. "I didn't mean to bug you." Her face was calm, but her left hand, clenching her purse strap, was trembling. "Sorry." She swept out of the front door, closing it behind her.

And she was gone. Out the door, out of my life. Thank goodness. I shuddered, shaking my shoulders, as I ran over to the door and flipped the lock. Alfie would have to knock when he returned. He wouldn't believe this!

I tried to put the entire encounter out of my mind, moving to resume my music. My records brought with them a sense of calm that I needed, a source of stress diffusion, which I could apply at the moment. A girl had just broken into my home. I scoffed at the notion.

Strangers could be so intrusive. I let a deep breath fill my lungs and dropped the needle.

Sk, sk, sk sk.

I felt my stomach drop, my heart trying to steady a quivering lip of its own. Wilting in disappointment, I listened to the record skip four times over and sighed deeply, removing it from the player and sliding it back into the case. It must have had a scratch after all.

About the Author

Hannah has a great passion for the creative arts, including writing, singing, acting, and drawing. She takes pride in her schoolwork and hopes to one day take an active role in government/law, possibly even use her writing skills to achieve her goals. She doesn't know exactly where she's heading yet, but she finds comfort in expressing herself creatively and delving into popular culture for inspiration. Though Hannah is young, she loves to contemplate how the world works and try to understand things from other people's perspectives, something she often incorporates into her writing. She is honored and excited to be recognized, and hopes her short story will offer some empathy on the topics of Alzheimer's and Dementia.

Teen Published Finalist

Glass Slippers
Kevina Clear

Glass slippers are all very well for dancing, but running? Not so much.

One had stayed behind on the palace steps, but there was no time to go back for it. I hurried into the waiting coach and ripped off my ballgown, revealing my torn, stained dress underneath. I tied my hair up in a red kerchief and climbed out the other side of the coach. The courtyard was filled with coaches of every color. I ducked behind one and glanced around, making sure there was no one to see me.

Tom drove the coach away at breakneck speed, clattering the cobblestones. He'll be alright. I hope.

Thundering hoofbeats signaled the arrival of the King's Guard. All this for me? Who do they think I am? Aunt Lily hadn't wanted me to come to the castle. She'd said it was too dangerous. Was this why? It doesn't matter, I reminded myself. Leaving Father locked up in the castle dungeons was far more dangerous. It had been months since the guards had arrested him at that inn. By now, he could be...no. I refused to think that.

When I had told the king my name was Elnora, his eyes filled with an emotion I didn't recognize. Tom had said it would affect him, but I hadn't understood. I still didn't understand. When I find Father, he'll explain.

The guards rode by, taking no notice of the ragged servant girl.

I walked around to the back of the castle. As soon as I sidled through the kitchen door, a ladle came flying at my head.

"Where have you been, you lazy girl?" the head cook shrieked. "These sandwiches should've gone up fifteen minutes ago."

"Sorry, Mrs. Burm," I mumbled, taking the tray.

I carried them out into the hallway, but instead of turning right, toward the ballroom, I turned left. The way to the dungeons.

The farther I went, the rougher-hewn the walls became, with fewer lamps to light the way. At a particularly dark spot, I pulled a small flask from my pocket and dropped some liquid onto each sandwich. I slipped it back into my pocket and went on.

Soon, I reached the first pair of guards.

I held the tray toward them. "Mrs. Burm sent these, as you're missing the festivities." "I'd prefer wine," said one.

They laughed, and I joined in.

When they'd each taken a sandwich, I moved along the passageway to the next set of guards.

I made my way in this fashion until I reached the dungeons. More guards milled about here. I looked at my tray of sandwiches. Would there be enough?

I clapped my hands to get everyone's attention. "Good sirs," I cried, "Mrs. Burm desired that you all should have a taste of the festivities, as you cannot be there."

They all came and took some sandwiches. I looked at each guard, hoping to see a ring of keys dangling from one's waist. No one had them.

I stopped the last man to come up and asked him, "Are there more guards this way?" I pointed toward the deeper part of the dungeons.

"Just the jailer," he replied, his mouth full.

I thanked him and walked away, past the cells barred with iron. I turned the corner and there he was. The jailer. Tall and wide, he looked solid enough to stop a bolting horse in its tracks.

"Hello, sir," I said, summoning a smile. "Mrs. Burm sends her compliments along with these sandwiches."

"I don't eat sandwiches," he growled. "Some wine, perhaps?"

"I don't drink on the job." He folded his massive arms across his chest.

"Not even a little sip? Surely that wouldn't render you witless." Please, you must want something.

"No," he admitted. "But I won't do it."

All would be for naught if I couldn't get the keys. Desperate, I said, "What if I get you a nice chicken leg?"

He relented. "Alright."

Inwardly, I sighed with relief. "I'll get it right now." I didn't know how, but I'd get it.

As I hurried back through the passageway, I noticed the guards starting to look a little groggy.

Good. The drug was already taking effect. The first set of guards looked ready to pass out.

When I reached the kitchen, Mrs. Burm glared at me. "That took long enough. These tarts are getting cold."

Dutifully, I took the platter and turned toward the ballroom. My stomach was churning with anxiety. If the jailer wondered why everyone had gone so quiet and investigated, he'd see all the unconscious guards and my plans were foiled. For that matter, if anyone went down there I'd be in huge trouble.

At the door to the ballroom, I handed the tray to one of the footmen who carried the food into the ballroom.

"If there are any empty platters of chicken, I'll take them back with me." I tried to sound casual but my heart was ready to beat out of my chest. "Even if there's one or two pieces left, I'll take it. It's not a good look to have empty trays."

He nodded. "I'll check."

I tapped my foot on the stone floor. Every moment that passed was a moment closer to when the drug would wear off. I don't have time for this.

After what seemed like an eternity, the footman returned bearing a platter on which rested— wonder of wonders—a beautiful chicken leg.

"Thank you," I said, with more enthusiasm than he likely expected. I wrapped it in my kerchief and slipped it into my pocket.

When I reached the kitchen, I thrust the tray into the hands of a maid going in and turned to go back to the dungeons, sprinkling the chicken liberally with sleeping draught as I walked. Hopefully more would give faster results.

In the dungeons, all the guards were lying on the floor, unconscious. I picked my way around them, finally reaching the jailer. He stood exactly as I had left him, arms folded across his chest.

"Here it is." I handed him the chicken.

He took it wordlessly and bit off a huge mouthful.

I left him to enjoy it alone. At least, that was the impression I wanted to give. My true purpose was to find a guard whose clothes I could steal. I found one who looked to be about Father's size and stripped off his helmet, hood, tunic, and pants.

When I returned, the jailer stood as he always had, solid and immovable. He glared at me. "What do you want now?"

Why wasn't the potion working? I reached into my pocket and felt around for something— anything—to buy time. My fingers closed around the glass slipper. "I forgot to give you this." Once I had seen a horse knock a man unconscious. If I hit just the right spot...

I pulled the slipper out of my pocket and slammed it into the back of his head. He crumpled to the ground.

I took his ring of keys and stared at the rows of cells. Which one held Father? "Father!" I called.

No answer came but the rattling of chains and the moaning of broken men.

I peered into a cell, but it was too dark to see if anyone was in it, let alone identify them.

"Father! Father!" I made my way through the block of cells, calling at every door. The prisoners inside ignored me. I supposed they were too wrapped up in their own pain to talk to a strange girl looking for her father.

"Father!" I grew frantic. What if he wasn't here? I thought I'd seen royal soldiers take him from the inn we were staying at, but maybe I was wrong. Or maybe the thought I'd pushed away for the past few months was true. Maybe he was…No! I won't give up.

I tried again. "Father?"

This time, a hoarse voice replied, "Ella?" "Father!" I ran toward his voice.

"What are you doing here?" He sounded haggard and worn.

I fumbled with the keys, searching for the one to fit the lock. "Getting you out, of course." "But…how did you find me?"

I tried a key in the lock. It didn't fit. "It was Tom, mostly. Your sister helped too." "Tom?"

I tried another key. "He's a coachman. He used to work for Mother's father when she was a girl." "Oh, old Tom. I remember him." His words dissolved into a fit of coughing.

Yet another key refused to fit. I shook the lock in frustration. "We need to get you out." "How?" he rasped. "There are too many guards."

"I drugged them, and I stole you this uniform." I picked up the clothes and tossed them through the iron bars. "Put it on while I get this door unlocked."

"I can't," he said. "I'm shackled to the floor."

"Oh." Another layer of difficulty. "Same key or different key?" "Different." He coughed. "I think."

Of course.

At last, a key turned in the lock. I threw open the door and flew to the dark corner where Father sat. I hugged him as if I'd never let go.

"I didn't know if I'd ever see you again," I whispered. "I never thought I would see you again."

When I pulled away, I saw his face. "What have they done to you?" Bruises and scrapes darkened his cheeks. His left eye was swollen shut. Every breath he took seemed to require a tremendous effort.

"Never mind now. Like you said, we need to get out."

I stroked his scraped cheek, then set to work finding the key for his restraints. This time, I was lucky. The second key I tried was the right one. First, I unshackled his ankles. The skin was raw and bleeding where the iron cuffs had cut into his legs.

My stomach clenched. "Oh, Father. Can you stand?" "I won't know until I try."

I freed his wrists, then, slowly, I helped him to his feet. He was shaky, but he could stand. He took a few halting steps forward and almost fell over.

I shook my head. "You'll never pass for a guard. No one could think you're anything but a prisoner."

So that was what he'd have to be.

I ripped the skirt off my dress and pulled off my petticoats, leaving just my pantaloons. I stepped into the guard's pants, tugged the tunic over my bodice, then slipped the chain mail hood over my head.

I turned back to Father. "I don't know how long we have before the guards come to. We need to hurry."

"Wait, Ella." He grabbed my arm and stared deep into my eyes. "What have they told you?"

"Aunt Lily and Tom?" I exhaled sharply. "Not nearly enough. Tom's favorite phrase is 'It's not my story to tell.'" I slid the shackles back around his wrists, not locking them. "I expect you to explain everything when we're safe, but we don't have time now. Come on."

We walked out of the cell—that is, I walked. Father dragged himself along, leaning on me.

"All we have to do is get off the castle grounds," I whispered. "Aunt Lily has horses waiting for us."

He nodded. I could see it took all his energy just to put one foot in front of the other. Hands reached through the bars of the cells, grabbing at me as I passed.

"How about letting us out?"

"Just toss the keys in here, that's all you have to do." I shook my head, trying to ignore them.

We made it to the jailer. I put his keys back where I'd found them, then we continued on our way.

It was painfully slow going. Every few steps, Father had to stop and catch his breath. His knees seemed ready to collapse under him.

I led him around unconscious guards, praying fervently they'd stay that way. Every moment, I expected one to wake up and question us.

Finally, I could see the first set of guards. The door to freedom was just after them. "We're almost there," I tried to encourage Father.

His only reply was a half-smile.

When we'd almost reached the guards, one of them stirred and sat up. My heart stopped.

"Father," I hissed," I know it's hard, but we need to get out now." His pace increased minutely.

The guard's eyes wandered around the hall. I stared straight ahead, willing him to not notice us. His eyes rested on me.

"You there," he slurred. "What's going on?" I racked my brain for an answer. Deflect.

"Have you been drinking?" I asked, attempting to deepen my voice. It came out sounding like a donkey with a sore throat.

"No!"

"But you've been sleeping on the job," I accused. "I ought to report you." Just a few more feet and we'd be outside.

"So's he!" The guard pointed to his still-unconscious partner. "There must have been something in those sandwiches."

"Sounds like you need to take it up with the kitchen staff, then."

"You're right." He tried to stand, then collapsed to the floor. "After I... wake...up." His eyelids fluttered shut.

I let out the breath I'd been holding in.

At last, we reached the door. I pulled it open and we stepped into the fresh night air.

Father slid to the ground against the wall, his chest heaving.

I looked around, my ears straining for the thundering of hoofbeats. How long could Tom's distraction work? All I heard was the far-off strains of music from the ballroom, the fluttering of flags in the breeze, and the distant sounds of the city.

Father broke the quiet. "You know, this isn't the first time we've had to run for our lives from this castle."

I stared at him. "Really?"

He nodded. "When you were a baby, your mother and I had to flee." But... he'd never told me this.

"Why were you here?"

He smiled. "We lived here. You were born here."

My voice grew hushed. "Father, what are you saying?"

"You're a princess, Ella. Your mother was the king's daughter. She should have been queen after him, but when he died, this pretender," he gestured toward the castle, "stole the throne."

I felt like I'd been run over by a team of oxen. "So," I stammered, "I should be queen?" "Yes."

It didn't make sense. And yet, it did.

It explained the change that came over King Percival's face when I told him my name, Tom's secrecy, and Aunt Lily's reluctance to let me go to the castle. It was why the guards had taken Father away.

The guards.

I snapped out of my trance. "We need to go."

I helped Father to his feet, and we started across the courtyard. I looked back at the castle.

My castle.

One day, I vowed, I'll be back.

I didn't know how, or when, or who would help me. But I knew that this was where I belonged. This was where I could make a difference in the lives of everyone in the kingdom.

This was my home.

About the Author

Kevina Clear is a 16-year-old bibliophile, hailing from the southwest corner of the grand ole' Mitten State, where she has resided for all of her rich years on her family's mini farm. Her love for books and reading started early: she read J.R.R. Tolkien's "The Hobbit" before she turned five. She wrote her first story at age six and has moved on to write numerous short stories and novels, including a seven-book series. When she isn't writing, she enjoys multiple hobbies, including many types of crafting, in addition to her love for gardening and botany. She grows artisan lettuces for the organic salads she devotedly makes for her very large and musical family. She plays the piano in her free time, and is currently working on mastering the tin whistle, while also learning Irish, French, and Latin, plus working on math courses for school. Kevina is very passionate about the earth and sustainability and sees herself possibly working in small-scale organic farming in the future.

Teen Published Finalist
The Littlest Chickadee
Grace Jacobson

"The family is one of nature's masterpieces." George Santayana.

I watch as chickadees and cardinals greedily raid the bird feeder and then chirp happily as they fly away.

My easel and paints lay next to me as I'm mesmerized by the birds. Although I feel a smile ghost my face—I still can not bring myself to paint anything. Something, or should I say someone, is missing and has taken my ability to capture the beauty in a painting, away with them.

The feeling of emptiness has been growing stronger over time but I've been finding comfort in the birds. They are not afraid of anything. They are free and they seem to enjoy spreading their wings and learning to fly.

One lone chickadee comes to rest on the feeder and he pecks the seed. It falls to the ground and he watches it before flapping his wings and swooping down to catch it. He takes the seed in his beak and then flies away.

I turn to my easel and look at the outline of the chickadee. My inspiration has faded away so I take my paintbrushes and begin to put them away.

"No, Dale. You should talk to her." I hear my parents quietly talking outside the door and I sigh softly.

A few minutes later, my dad awkwardly enters the room. "Hey Luna. Your mom and I were wondering if you would like to go out and see a movie."

I shake my head and tuck my brushes inside my box of painting supplies. My dad exhales and sticks his hands in his pockets.

He seems to be at a loss for words as he looks around the room. Old paintings I've done over the years, hang on the walls. Chickadees and cardinals stare back at me as I close the lid of my box.

Finally I smile and say, "Maybe another time?" Dad sighs and nods his head, not wanting to push me. He squeezes my shoulder before slowly leaving the room.

I know how badly my parents want to help me but grief is something you kind of have to get over yourself. Try as they might—I have to get over this myself. While I appreciate their support I still need to do this myself.

After setting my supplies back on the shelf, I leave the craft room and go to my bedroom.

Without thinking about it, I pull my memory box from my closet and open it up. I take out an envelope and pull out a worn letter.

My dearest Luna, it reads, my little chickadee. With your midnight black hair and warm brown eyes, you remind me of the tiny bird. They always were my favorite, as were you.

Tears prick at my eyes as I read my grandfather's fond words. He continues to fill the paper with sentences filled with love. I hear his gentle voice read the words to me, even though I'm the one reading the letter.

Continue to paint my little chickadee. You have a gift, even though you are too modest to admit it. You capture not only the beauty of the moment but you capture the memory as well.

When my grandfather passed away, I felt this emptiness that I had never felt before. The thing is...I'd always thought my grandpa was invincible.

Grandpa was my hero—he was my number one supporter but he was also my closest confidant. I thought he would be around forever.

I know you'll make me proud no matter what you do. You have to spread your wings and fly, my chickadee. You will do great things in life, I just know it. I smile sadly and hug the letter to my chest.

Grandpa loved writing almost as much as he loved taking pictures. Although nothing could truly rival his love of photography.

He said it was often easier for him to put his thoughts on paper. He said it was easier for him to express himself through written words rather than spoken ones.

Before he passed away, he wrote everyone in our family a letter. It was his way of saying goodbye—on his own terms.

I sit down at my desk and reach into my bottom drawer. I take out a piece of paper and my favorite ballpoint pen.

Dear Grandpa, I begin, It has been four months since we last saw each other. I try to do as you say and spread my wings, but it is not easy.

I crumple up the ball of paper and toss it in my waste basket. I know what I want to say but I can't quite find the right words. How do you express months worth of frustration, sadness, emptiness, and loneliness in a piece of paper?

My knee bounces up and down as I search for what I want to say and how I want to say it. I look out my window and see the same small chickadee from before. He chirps at me and flutters his wings, but instead of flying away, he stays right where he is. He remains on the feeder hanging outside the bedroom window.

I notice that his feathers are slightly ruffled. He chirps again and tilts his small head to the side. I smile at him and softly hum to myself.

"Perhaps you can help me, Mr.Chickadee." I murmur. He just chirps and pecks at the seeds. I sigh and attempt to focus once more on my paper.

Chirp. Chirp. Chirp. I look up and see the tiny bird has scooted even closer to my window. He blinks his dark eyes and shakes out his feathers.

Of all the chickadees I've seen this year, he is by far the littlest one. He has the darkest eyes and pretty feathers—he reminds me of a painting in a bird book. Perfect yet too perfect to exist.

He flaps his little wings and rises up in the air before returning to his spot on the bird feeder. He blinks once more and chirps.

"Why you are a little chatterbox." I say. A laugh escapes before I can stop it and it catches me by surprise. I look at the small bird and shake my head.

Then all of sudden he takes off and flies across the yard—chirping as he goes. I sigh and return my attention to writing my letter.

Thinking of the littlest chickadee, I pick up my pen and start to write. This time all the right words come to me.

Dear Grandpa,

It has been four months since we last saw each other. I haven't been painting lately because I've felt as if something is missing. Turns out what I was missing was you. I miss our weekend trips to the lake to watch birds and take pictures. I wish we could have one more conversation or share one more cup of cocoa. Because without you...life feels so empty. But when I see the birds, I think of you and all the happy memories we made. It makes me smile and forget about the grief. And I think I might be ready to start painting again. Perhaps it's time for me to spread my wings and learn to fly. Even if it means flying solo for a while. Because your little chickadee wants to make you proud. I can't express myself with words the way you can, nor can I express myself with pictures. But I can paint...I can capture the memories. I saw this tiny chickadee today and it made me think of myself. I am the littlest chickadee of the flock—I get lost in our big family. But with my paintings, I'm able to be more than quiet little Luna. I'm able to be me. And so grandpa, I am finally ready to spread my wings and fly. I'll never stop missing you and I'll never forget our times together. I'm thankful for all of it because it helped make me into the person I am today. I miss you and I hope to make you proud. Love, your little chickadee, Luna.

I carefully fold the piece of paper and stick it inside of an envelope. I write my grandpa's name in neat cursive on the front of the envelope, before tucking it in my pocket.

I go downstairs and find my parents in the kitchen. I hesitantly smile and ask, "Would one of you be able to give me a ride?"

Both agree to accompany me to the cemetery. A comfortable silence falls over the car, as we all keep to ourselves. Soft snowflakes fall through the air and I smile. On days like these, grandpa and I would go out and bird watch. The snow and winter weather brings back happy memories—instead of sadness. Which means I'm making progress. My grief won't disappear overnight but it won't hang over me all the time. I can think of happy times instead.

When we arrive at the cemetery, I get out and go to my grandpa's grave. I take the envelope out of my pocket and hold it in my hands. I smile and set it down by his grave. "For you Grandpa." I look around and memorize every detail of my beautiful surroundings, knowing when I get home I will sit down and sketch it out. Then I will paint it.

As I turn to leave, I see a flash of black and white fly by me. A smile creeps onto my face as I realize—it is the littlest chickadee. I wave at the bird and smile. He cheerfully chirps in reply, before flying away. Goodbye little chickadee.

About the Author

Grace is a fourteen year old with a love for reading and writing. With the support and encouragement of her two teachers, Mr.Chatel and Ms.Clairday, she was encouraged to further her passion for writing. She has always had an interest in writing, but it was with the support of these two teachers that she became more confident in her writing, and grew to love it even more. She hopes to continue to further her passion for writing in the future. She dreams of one day becoming a published author.

Teen Published Finalist

The Body in the Creek
Kate Zalapi-Bull

When I was a young teenager in Massachusetts, there was a group of us boys who became a bit famous for all the wrong reasons. It was the summer of '93, and there were five of us: Mason, Luke, Ryan, Elliot, and me, Jamie. Young and unable to comprehend just how dangerous the world could be, we spent that summer scraping our knees on the rocky hills and bruising our thighs on the branches of great oak trees. We were a little solar system in the hills of New England, our own unlikely little congregation, and Mason was our fearless leader.

Handsome in that thirteen-year-old way that only promised more to come, we willingly followed Mason everywhere he went. His father was the sheriff, so he had some clout to wave over our heads as well as being charming, confident, tall, and - well, let's just say he was superior to us in almost every way.

Next in the hierarchy was Luke, Mason's friend since long before the rest of us came along. He was quiet, more reserved than Mason could ever be. He was lankier too, long-limbed like a praying mantis, good for reaching the highest shelf in the pantry. But he rivaled Mason in smarts; where Mason was bold and always eager for attention, Luke was level-headed and closed off.

Then, there were Ryan and I, who were on pretty equal footing. I was what my mother fondly called 'a late bloomer' with baby fat still clinging to my cheeks and a soft, pale stomach. Ryan was fitted with braces as soon as his baby teeth were gone, and had a laugh like a seagull. The two of us were more skilled with video games and comics than girls.

And then there was Elliot. Elliot, naive and shy, never able to stand up for himself, was our devoted lackey. He was an easy target for bullying, as short and skinny as he was. Of course Luke was skinny too, but he was lean and slender, his muscles compact, which made him a good runner later on. Elliot was skinny like his growth had been stunted. He had eyes like Bambi, behind the coke-bottle lenses of his glasses, and a perpetual quiver to his mouth, like he was always on the verge of tears.

Looking back on it, we were probably too hard on Elliot most of the time. He was our friend, and we cared about him but we weren't his parents. We weren't mean like the other kids were, but we didn't baby him. Mason said it was only to toughen him up and of course, we followed Mason's every order. So we made it very clear to him that he could only hang out with us if he could keep up.

Anyhow, the five of us spent almost every day together that summer. Almost.

It was July, one particular week when the air was heavy with summer heat and the sky was flame blue and cloudless. When it gets that hot, there's nothing much to do other than turn on the air conditioning unit in your window and lay down on the floor. But Mason had other ideas, and he wasn't going to take no for an answer. So he dragged us all out of our houses and onto our bikes and we rode through town, wind in our hair and sun in our eyes.

Other kids took to the county pool or to the arcade to escape the heat, but we preferred the forest. It was quiet there, and we were free to be ourselves. When we were in those woods, beneath that shimmering canopy of green, it felt like nothing bad would happen to us. It felt like maybe my mother wasn't an alcoholic or Mason's dad didn't hit him, like Luke's sister was still alive or Ryan's parents didn't wish for a girl instead, and like Elliot wasn't crying all the time.

We loved that forest; we worshipped it.

I don't remember each second of what we did that day, but nothing we did was out of the ordinary. That day we parked our bikes at the edge of the woodlands, disappeared between the tree trunks, and left before dusk. We caught minnows and frogs in the creek and climbed so high into the trees we became kings instead of five lonely kids who needed each other more than we thought.

The only reason the day sticks out to me is because it was the last day I saw Elliot - the real Elliot - alive.

The next day, he was gone. His mother called the police around five in the morning, reporting her son missing from his bed and the back door open. There were no signs of a struggle. His glasses were still on the nightstand. No suspects, no clues, just an empty bed that had been occupied the night before. Mason's father said it was the most confusing case he'd come across in years. His theory was that Elliot had run away in the middle of the night, while his mother slept. The police told his mother not to panic until at least 24 hours had passed.

But we knew better.

Elliot was anything but a rebellious teenage runaway. His mother adored him and could never bear to neglect him. And even if she did, he would never be bold enough to attempt an escape. He was afraid of things like the dark and getting the flu. He never stayed outside past sunset. He cried whenever he scraped his knees. He didn't run away.

Hours passed. Then days. Then a week. I helped the others put up flyers on every telephone pole and shop window in town. We showed the police all of Elliot's favorite places to visit, from the creek to the rock quarry to the arcade. He was nowhere to be found. Gone, like he hadn't existed. Another week passed.

Those two weeks he was gone were the darkest two weeks of my young life.

Then, despite the statistics of missing children, despite the rule of the first forty-eight hours, Elliot was found. Or rather, he just showed up. Two weeks after his initial disappearance, Elliot walked barefoot out of the forest, clad only in his pajamas, all the way into town. The owner of the general store was just opening up for the day when he saw Elliot walking down the middle of the road. The owner called the police, and soon the whole town was awake.

Our neighborhood was swamped with news vans and police cars for the next couple of days. Reporters bombarded his mother with questions and shoved cameras in her face as she cried tears of joy. The townspeople thanked their lucky stars that Elliot managed to come home safely, like any one of them had cared about him before he vanished. I remember watching on television as the reporters swamped him with questions. But when they asked the question everyone was wondering, he could only produce one answer:

"I don't remember anything."

He was sent to therapists and psychologists, but his answer remained the same. Nothing anyone did seemed to jog his memory. Doctors examined him from head to toe and couldn't find a single scratch or bruise on him. It was like he had never disappeared in the first place.

So the experts looked the other way and said he was in shock and left it at that. It's not like anyone cared either way; after he came home, all the excitement died down and the story wasn't as interesting anymore. The news vans dispersed, and the reporters stopped knocking at our doors. Even his mother was just happy to have him home, no matter how he got back.

But behind the cameras, behind the backs of the public, I knew something was wrong.

His mother may not have noticed, but I did. Ever since I'd set my eyes on him, I knew he wasn't the Elliot I had known. It wasn't the kind of thing you could easily explain; he looked and sounded like himself, but the air around him seemed different. Before, people barely took notice of him. People hadn't even heard his name until it was on those missing posters.

But the Elliot that had come back could not be ignored. He demanded to be seen. When he walked into the room, people knew; just like they'd feel a chill down their spine from an open window. His eyes, which had once been soft and always aimed at his feet, now bore straight into others' with a darkness that only came from witnessing something unspeakable. His shadow darkened doorways, and his voice made blood run cold. And he reeked. He smelled like dirt and wet leaves, like a dead animal, like rot and decay and mold.

But I didn't want to avoid him, so I kept my feelings to myself. I thought I was the only one who noticed a difference in him, and my mother told me it was normal to feel complicated emotions after something so traumatic. And he was one of my best friends, and I had missed him more than anything. The weeks he was missing were the worst weeks of my life. I was so happy to have my friend back.

I wanted to be there for him if he needed me. And even if they were bad at showing it, I knew it was what the others wanted as well. So a few days after he returned, we tried to have a normal day together, just the five of us. I had been so excited to finally be with all of them again. Luke had even packed us lunch so we could stay out as long as we wanted.

But as soon as we approached the edge of town, Elliot became anxious. Not anxious like he usually was, but anxious like we were leading him to a slaughterhouse. He wouldn't get within five feet of the edge of the woods, and he outright refused to go hiking with us. We tried to convince him he was safe with us, and then he got angry. The anger on his face scared me that day. He looked into my eyes, and I felt my heart stop in my chest. I didn't recognize those eyes.

I wouldn't have admitted it at the time, but the new Elliot scared me.

So we rode back home and just hung out around his house for the rest of the day. It was fine; we were happy to do that too.

I rode home that day feeling much worse about the situation with Elliot. He didn't look like himself, and he didn't sound like himself either. He was scary. When he'd looked at me that day, my body kicked into a fight or flight response. I'd felt like I was staring into the eyes of an angry predator. Other than him acting completely out of character, I couldn't put my finger on why he'd scared me so badly. It was like trying to remember a dream after you've woken up from it.

It was well into the night, just before I fell asleep, when I finally figured it out. Elliot had blue eyes.

That day, they'd been black.

§

In the weeks that followed, we saw less and less of Elliot. July turned to August, and with it, those suffocatingly hot temperatures that came with the height of summer began to weaken. I spent my days in my room with the windows open, and on the back porch with glasses of ice tea as the sun set over the trees. The five of us got together only a few times since he'd gotten home, and then Elliot became a bit of a recluse. There were times when we'd wait on his porch only for his mother to come out and tell us he didn't feel like playing today.

So it was just the four of us again. I only saw Elliot around town, and a few other times when he was out in his yard. And then another week passed, and I didn't see him at all. Luke told us he probably just needed space, and none of us wanted to consider any different reasons for his behaviour. So we stopped knocking on Elliot's door and instead spent our time on my back porch, playing card games and drinking cherry cola, as we dreaded the upcoming school year.

Then, one day near the tail-end of August, Mason called my house in the early hours of the morning. Dawn was just breaking over the hills when he told me to come as fast as I could to the woods. There was panic in his voice. I threw on my shoes without question and pedaled over, still in my pajamas. As I was nearing the edge of town, two police cars came whipping right past me going in the same direction. My heart crawled into my throat. I pedaled harder.

When I neared the woods, red and blue flashing lights came into view. I felt like I was going to throw up. I saw my friend's bikes discarded in the dirt, spokes facing upward. I dropped my own bike onto the ground and stared at the crowd of officers standing at the forest's edge. The sheriff, Mason's father was there, and he was consoling a crying woman who I later realized was Elliot's mother. Next to them was another officer, kneeling on the ground, zipping up a large black bag. My legs started to tremble as I approached them.

Mason, Luke, and Ryan pushed through the crowd when they spotted me. They were all in their pajamas. Luke was pale and Ryan had obviously been crying. I broke into a run.

Mason caught me just as I fell to the ground and started to sob. I started to sob because I knew who was in that bag, I think I had known all along. I had known for a month.

I watched as officers put the bag on a metal stretcher, and loaded it into the back of an ambulance. There was a news van coming down the road. The sun was climbing higher into the sky. The sheriff held Elliot's mother by her arm as they closed the van doors and said something to her that I managed to hear just as the officers ushered us away.

I wish I'd never heard him.

A couple of hikers had found Elliot's body, rotted and bloated and decomposing in the creek. According to the decay, his body had been there for almost a month.

About the Author

Kate is a senior at North Farmington High School. As an honors student, she's been active in marching and concert band as well as the theatre program. She loves books and movies, and aspires to be an author and screenwriter one day. Although she loves all genres, her all time favorite is horror and mystery. After graduation Kate will be attending Michigan State Univeristy in the Residential College of Arts and Humanities.

Judges' Choice Youth Winner

Adventures in Fairy Land
Emerson Gerard

Once upon a time, there was a little girl and boy. Their names were Emerson (or Em), and Cohen. They were brother and sister. They lived in a place called Evil, (sounds pretty evil, right?) where they lived under the rule of an evil queen. And no, she's not the evil queen from Snow White. They are many evil queens, okay? Anyway, the Evil Queen, as they call her, lived in a huge, thorny, dark magenta, full-of-poison-ivy-on-the-outside, palace. Everyone within the town worked for her.

Every day when the loud, gonging bells would go off at 5:00 in the morning, the townspeople would have to walk down the muddy path to the palace, where they spent the whole day doing chores, and other boring stuff for the Evil Queen. Then, at 10:00, every evening they would walk home and go to bed. Everyone in the town had a very small, gross, wood, full of bugs, hut, with hay for sleeping on, a well for water, and outside of their house, a porta potty. They each had one pair of clothes: a ragged brown shirt and ragged brown pants. Every day at 7:00 a.m., and 8:00 p.m., they would be given brown stew to eat: and don't even ask what was in there.

One day it was just like any other day. DING! DONG! DING! DONG! The morning bells seemed to howl as loud as they possibly could.

"Ugh. 5:00 in the morning is way too early for a 4 and 5 year old kid to wake up." sighed Em.

"Yeah! I'm only 4!". agreed Cohen. "Oh. And also you say that every morning Em."

"I know, but it's true!: Come on, let's brush our teeth and hurry down to the palace." said Em. They quickly brushed their teeth and ran down the muddy path to the palace as fast as they could. "The...least...she...could do... is give...us...shoes!" Em panted, trying to catch her breath.

"Yeah! My feet are cold!" agreed Cohen. They walked up the palace steps, trying as hard as they could to step around the thorns and poison ivy. Two guards were there, dressed in dark magenta, with a tall, fuzzy, black hat, and long, shiny, pointy, and scary weapons.

"Name." demanded one of the guards.

"Emerson and Cohen Gerard." answered Emerson.

The other guard looked down at a sheet of paper and then said, "The queen's waiting for you" as he pushed open the palace doors. Em and Cohen walked into the palace and wiped their feet on the magenta rug. They quickly ran to the kitchen and started working right away.

"You get the milk and sugar!" Em said to Cohen as she quickly put a teapot on the stove. They gathered up many ingredients and then put them into the teapot and poured the tea into a small, black, teacup, then hurried over and put the teacup onto a silver tray, and hurried upstairs to the ballroom, where the Evil Queen was sitting on her huge, dark magenta, spiky throne.

"Your tea, your majesty." said Emerson as she balanced the tray while bowing down. Cohen forgot to bow and just stood there.

"You disgusting little child." said the Evil Queen. "You're so stupid you don't even know to bow in the presence of a queen." spat the Evil Queen.

"S-so sorry your majesty. I'm so sorry," stuttered Cohen as he quickly bowed. Ah man! Not again! Emerson thought to herself.

"Give me my tea," said the Evil Queen with a snarl. Emerson walked over and handed the Evil Queen her tea. "Now go sweep the kitchen. After that you shall wash the dishes. Then you shall report back to me. Now shoo!" demanded the Evil Queen. Emerson and Cohen walked out of the room as the Evil Queen muttered "Dirty little rats."

As soon as there was no one around and they knew the Evil Queen couldn't hear them, Emerson started lecturing Cohen on how he has to bow when in the presence of the queen. "I can't believe you forgot again!" exclaimed Em.

"I know! I know! I'm sorry! I didn't mean to. I don't know why I forget! I just get so scared in front of her that I just forget what to do!" Cohen sputtered, looking ashamed of himself.

"I know. I get scared too but you just have to remember! Who knows what she'll do to us if you forget too many times!" said Emerson.

"Okay. Sorry." Cohen apologized. "I just don't get how mom and dad liked her.

I'm glad we escaped from them." "Me too" agreed Em.

Later that day Emerson and Cohen walked to their hut after a long day of hard work. "Whew! That was one tiring day!" said Em as she opened the door to their hut.

"Yeah!" agreed Cohen.

"Now come on! Let's practice what you do in the presence of the Evil Queen." "Aaaaw! But we just got home!" said Cohen with a sad look on his face." "Yeah well you need to learn to remember. And if you don't, then who knows?

She might put us in The Prison."

"Aaaaah!" screamed Cohen. "Not The Prison! B-b-b-but you barely get any food in there and they poke you with spikes and they don't let you sleep and it's soooooooo tiny!" exclaimed Cohen.

"Exactly," said Em. "You don't want us to get put in there, do you? That's why you need to practice your bowing. You think I want to do this? No! Obviously I don't but it's for the best," said Em.

"Yeah. I guess." agreed Cohen.

Later that night, Emerson and Cohen decided that it was about time that they go to bed. But when Emerson walked over to go onto her hay bed she thought she smelled something: and it stunk! "What is that smell?" Em wondered aloud. "Do you smell that?!?" she asked Cohen.

"No!" said Cohen.

Em walked over to the hay and pushed it to the side. "What the..." There was a big black hole under the hay. She leaned in to get a closer look when all of a sudden... she fell. "AAAAAAAAAAHH!" she screamed as she fell down the hole. It was pitch black and she couldn't see anything! Then, after what seemed like hours, she landed on a huge mushroom with a thump! "Owww!" she said as she rubbed the bruise on her head.

She rolled off the mushroom and onto the ground where she then rolled under the mushroom. Then she got up, looked around: and fainted. A few hours later she woke up to someone shaking her. "Wake up! Wake up!" someone called as they shook her. Emerson woke up and found someone leaning very close to her face.

"Cohen?" she asked.

"No! Not Cohen! Me!" said someone. She opened her eyes all the way and saw the person who was shaking her.

"Aaaaaah!" she screamed. "Y-y-y-you have wings! Y-y-y-your a fairy!"

"Uhh. Duuuh." said the fairy. "Are you okay?" the fairy asked, not seeming to know how surprised Emerson was.

"Yeah. I'm fine." she answered. "Oh no! Where's Cohen? Where am I? Who are you?!?"

"Cohen's at my house, you're in Fairy Land, and I'm Daisy." answered the fairy.

Em got up off of the mushroom and realized that her back felt kind of funny. She then turned around and saw something sparkly on her back. "Aaaaaaahh! I have wings!" yelled Emerson.

"Yeah," said Daisy calmly. "All girls have wings, and all boys have staffs. You got a lot to learn-wait. What's your name?"

"Emerson."

"Well. You've got a lot to learn Emerson," said Daisy. Daisy led Emerson through a forest to her house so that Emerson could see Cohen. Emerson always knew exactly where Daisy was (even though Daisy was moving very quickly) because of her bright white dress with some sort of belt that was yellow. Em followed Daisy and eventually they arrived at Daisy's house. It was a very big mushroom with a door at the base.

Daisy led Em inside and Em heard someone yell her name. "Emerson!" yelled a familiar voice.

"Cohen!" Em went over to see her brother. He was carrying a shiny silver staff almost the size of him. "Oh my gosh I have sooooo much to tell you!" said a very excited Emerson.

"Me too!" responded Cohen. As they ate some of the most delicious food ever, (mushroom soup) Em and Cohen told each other their stories. "And then I yelled: "Em!" and I didn't know what happened! So I ran over and dived in after you! The falling part was fun! It was scary that you couldn't see anything though!"

"I know right!" agreed Emerson.

"And then I got off the mushroom and started looking around! But I went right past you!"

"Wait-" said Daisy, "So just to clarify, you guys lived in Evil, under the rule of the Evil Queen?"

"Yeah." said Em. "Wait-you know who she is?"

"Yeah. All fairies do. One time she escaped from her home because her parents didn't treat her well. She somehow ended up here. For some reason-we think it might have been because she was angry, and believe me, no other fairy has ever really been very, very, angry-she didn't have wings. So she wanted us to get her wings, but we didn't know how. So then she started to figure out magic and made herself a wand, where she then made a castle, and ever since, she's wanted revenge because we "betrayed" her." said Daisy.

"Do you think that she'll attack Fairy Land?" asked Em with a hint of worry in her voice.

"I don't really know," sighed Daisy. "Well, it's best you be off. You need to learn to live on your own and explore Fairy Land." said Daisy.

"Wait, we have to leave? Noooo but Daisy!" said Em.

"I'm sorry but you need to learn the way the world works in Fairy Land and it's best that you figure out some of it yourselves. I'm not fit for a mom, or a babysitter.

Sorry kids. Here's a basket with some food and clothing. Goodbye children. I'm very sorry." said Daisy sadly.

"Bye Daisy! Thank you so much for everything!" said the kids. "Bye." said Daisy softly as Em and Cohen walked out the door.

Em and Cohen walked for about an hour before they realized they were pretty hungry. "I'm starving!" said Cohen, as he marched and thumped his staff on the ground. (Em heard his stomach rumble.)

"Me too," sighed Em. "Let's find somewhere to eat." As they were walking Em saw something shiny on the ground. "What's this?" she wondered aloud as she picked it up. It was a beautiful, very shiny, acorn. "Woah!" she said as she put it in her pocket.

Em and Cohen picked up every one that they saw.

After a while Em and Cohen found a restaurant. They went inside and were filled with the familiar aroma of mushroom soup. The siblings looked around the restaurant in awe. The floor ws moss and there were all different kinds of plants growing everywhere. A big sign was at the front of the restaurant that read: Mushroom Cafe. Their waiter, a girl fairy around 18 years old Em guessed, led them to their table. (They both ordered the mushroom soup since they knew they liked it.) After Em and Cohen ate, Em realized something. "Oh no." she said. "We don't have any money to pay for this stuff."

The waiter came over and said, "Okay children. That'll be 12 acorns." "What?" asked Em, confused.

"You're gonna have to pay for that food you know." said their waiter grumpily. "12 acorns."

"Oh!" said Em happily. "The currency is acorns!" she said to Cohen.

"Oh!" said Cohen. They got the acorns out of their pockets and handed them to the grumpy waiter. All of a sudden the restaurant started rumbling. Things started crashing through the roof. Em and Cohen ran outside. The sky was swirling a dark magenta color and huge crystals were falling everywhere. Em and Cohen looked at each other with worried expressions on their faces. They were both thinking the same thing: the Evil Queen was attacking Fairy Land!

Em and Cohen ran as fast as they could. They eventually found a dark, shady area where they started talking. "If the Evil Queen sees us, then she'll attack us." said Em. "We need a disguise." Em and Cohen looked around the basket that Daisy had given them. They looked through it and eventually found some dark magenta cloaks. "I have an idea." said Em. She explained it to Cohen and they put on the cloaks and rubbed dirt on their faces. "Wait!" said Em. She grabbed a vine and aske Cohen to hold it. She then folded her wings and tied the vine around them. "Ow." she said.

"You don't have to do that," said Cohen.

"I know, but if it means that we can save Fairy Land, then a little pain's worth it." said Em. They left the basket and Cohen's staff and ran to where they were seeing big flashes of light.

They had guessed well. The Evil Queen was exactly where they thought. "Let's do this." exclaimed Em. The siblings ran toward the Evil Queen until they were right next to her. "Let's get rid of all these fairies." said Em to the Evil Queen. She and Cohen went over to the fairies.

"Good job." said the Evil Queen as Em and Cohen pretended to kick and punch different fairies, but really, it was the Evil Queen who was zapping them with her wand. After a while of this, Em walked over to the Evil Queen, who laughed every time she zapped a fairy, in which the fairy would fall to the ground into a deep sleep.

"Your majesty," said Em sweetly, "I think that I deserve a chance with the wand." she said.

"No!" yelled the Evil Queen. Emerson went over and grabbed the wand.

"I want a chance with the wand!" whined Emerson in the whiniest voice she could make. She then pulled up on the wand as hard as she possibly could... SNAP! The wand broke in two. Time seemed to stop. The sky stopped swirling. The crystals stopped falling. The Evil Queen started to turn pale.

"No." she whispered in a hoarse voice. "NOOOOOOOOOO!" she screamed and got tinier and tinier until she disappeared into a puff of smoke, and a big dark magenta wave sprung out, moving it's way all across fairy land and knocking every fairy it hit onto the ground. All the fairies who were sleeping woke up.

"We did it." said Em. "We did it! We did it! We did it!" her and Cohen yelled happily as they jumped up and down. "We actually defeated the Evil Queen!" Em and Cohen walked around and made sure everyone was okay, and then ran off to someplace special...

"Em! Cohen!" Daisy exclaimed when she opened the door to find the two kids standing there.

"Daisy!" they said together. They went into Daisy's house and told her the entire story.

"Yeah! I had found those cloaks in someone's trash can. I knew they would come of use! Wow! You two are so brave!" said Daisy, "Much braver than me. I'm very sorry. I didn't want you to be in my house for too long because I was afraid that if I was found by the Evil Queen with you, I would get attacked. I'm very sorry."

"It's okay Daisy!" said Cohen, "If you never would have kicked us out then we wouldn't have defeated the Evil Queen!" said Cohen excitedly. They all laughed at that comment.

After a few days at Daisy's house, they were finally ready. They had spent most of the time there training Em to use her wings so that she could fly her and Cohen back up the hole.

One morning they walked over to the mushroom that had started their magnificent adventure. "We'll miss you so much Daisy! Thank you so much for everything!" said Em and Cohen as they got on the mushroom.

"I'll miss you too, children." said Daisy.

"Bye!" said the kids as Em started flying up the hole, holding Cohen by his legs. "Bye! Visit soon!" Daisy called to them as they disappeared through the hole.

One morning when Em and Cohen were having a picnic in a field near their hut, (since the Evil Queen was gone they got to do whatever they wanted all day) Em felt something hit her head. "Ow." she said as she picked the thing out of her hair. It was a tiny little crystal. All of a sudden the sky started swirling and crystals started falling everywhere. "Wait-" said Em, "It's only been five months!" Her and Cohen looked at each other. And they were thinking the same thing: they had an evil queen to defeat.

About the Author

Emerson Gerard is in sixth grade at North Rockford Middle school. She has cats, a dog and a younger brother. She loves piano, soccer, and basketball. In school, she loves reading, writing, math, and science. She got the idea for Adventures in Fairy Land from a game she used to play with her brother.

Youth Judges' Choice Runner-Up

Star's Journey
Lillian Steilstra

"Hurry it up!!!" called Moon, a black horse with a perfect white stripe down her face and a star in the shape of a diamond on her forehead, also white.

"I don't feel much like running right now," I replied. My legs are already worn out from walking all those miles and running away from that ferocious pack of wolves. How do the others still have so much energy?

"Come on, it's fun!" She taunted me by running in front of my face and bucking on the way back to the others.

"No, thanks," I was exhausted. I noticed a horse hang back from the group as my eyelids started to droop and I got ready for a nap.

"He decided that he wants to rest, OK, Moon?" I heard my dad's booming voice. My dad was a chestnut bay Stallion, and the leader of the herd. He always said that it was the horses that made the land beautiful, but I never knew what he meant.

"Yes, Thunder. Leave him alone, Sterling!" I heard Moon's firm voice. The name Sterling immediately got my attention. My eyelids shot open, and I saw a dark dapple gray horse coming my way.

"Don't tell me what to do!" Sterling nickered angrily over his shoulder. I watched him warily as he advanced. He finally stopped in front of me.

"What do you want," I asked, trying to sound confident.

"I want you to come run with me, you filthy Leader's Pet," he demanded. "Now."

I felt my anger building up inside of me, and forced my ears to stay forward. I couldn't let him see how much I wanted to turn around and kick him right now! He knew my name was Star, and that I had a glossy black coat with a shining white star on my forehead.

"I'm good, but thanks for the offer. Maybe some other time, though," I answered camly. "You think you're so cool that you have a dad who's a leader, don't you? Well, that will all change, and you won't know what to do. You'll still cry out for your daddy, even when he's gone, defeated by another horse who took over the herd and banished him out of it. Won't you, leader's pet?" He spat the words in my face, and I felt a pang of hurt deep in my chest. All of a sudden, he lunged forward and gave me a quick, but hurtful, nip on my neck. Then he turned to leave. He got stopped short by a big, powerful, chestnut bay horse who had his ears pinned back against his head angrily. I was very frightened for a moment, thinking what Sterling had said was coming true, and that it was an intruder, here to take over the herd and challenge my dad. Then I realized it was my dad, and that fright got replaced by joy. He gave Sterling a nip on the neck, and Sterling reeled away from it, whinnying painfully.

"You're not as tough as you think you are, are you Sterling?" My dad asked in a furious voice. "I don't want to see you picking on my son again," and with that, he turned and left, leaving all the horses in amazement. I looked over and saw Moon smiling. As the horses dispersed around the meadow where we had stopped, she trotted over to me.

"Are you OK?" She asked, a worried tone in her voice. "Yeah, I'm fine. Thanks."

"He deserved that nip and talking to."

"Definitely, except he probably didn't learn his lesson. My dad might have to do a little more nipping to get through Sterling's big head!" We both laughed for a while.

"Hey, do you want to come play-fight with me?" Moon asked me, and I could feel her hopeful eyes bearing into mine.

"I guess. That nip definitely woke me up!" As we cantered over to a nice, fluffy patch of grass, I noticed Sterling walking over to us. I wanted to show him I didn't need my dad to stick up for me.

§

A few miles away to the north, a lone wolf, who was feared greatly by every animal within 100 miles because of his pure power and ferociousness, was resting on a large rock in his luxurious territory. His name was Asher, though he was called many different things by all the herds, packs, and flocks that knew how powerful he was. He was eating a deer that he had caught, and was about to move on to a rabbit, when he heard a horse whinnying. It sounded in pain!

"Perfect," He said to himself, "I'll eat some and save some! I haven't had a horse for dinner in a while. Maybe there'll even be a herd! Then I can get 2 or 3! Let's go hunting!" He leaped off his rock and started to track the enticing scent. It was heading south. He started to run as the scent got stronger.

§

"Hang on a moment, Moon." I pinned my ears back, flexed my muscles, and held my ground as Sterling came closer.

"What are you doing?" Moon whispered to me, and looked at me with a quizzical expression on her face. "Can't you see he's not here for a challenge? He's totally relaxed. He even has his head lowered in submission and remorse!"I had noticed this, too, and told her so. "I know, I'm just making sure. If I'm going to be leader someday, I might as well act like it!" I answered to her in a whisper. My voice was firm, but gentle. Sterling didn't even look at me as he approached. Instead, he looked at the ground. It was as if he was respecting me! He finally stopped and lifted his gaze to meet mine. I searched them for any signs of challenging or bullying. There was none. Only remorse and sorrow filled his eyes as he gazed at me apologetically.

"Yes?" I asked. I didn't dare let down my guard, in case he took advantage of it. I couldn't let those sad, apologetic eyes fool me!

"I just wanted to say that I'm sorry for the way I acted. I shouldn't have nipped you." "You wanted to, or were forced to?" Something changed in his eyes. Some of the remorse faded away, leaving anger.

"Listen, I'm only going to challenge you if you challenge me first!" His voice ripped through the tense air.

I snorted angrily and stomped my foot.

"I'm only challenging you because you challenged me first!" I shouted, which got everyone's attention. They all turned and gathered in a circle around us. I glanced over my shoulder and saw Moon looking anxiously back and forth between Sterling and I, but I was too furious to care. I was just about ready to give him as hard a fight as I possibly could.

"I've had enough of you making fun of me, challenging me, bullying me, and calling me a leader's pet! It's time we put this to an end, see who's more worthy of being leader someday!" I was so irritated and furious I didn't notice my dad as he made his way through the large circle of horses until he spoke up.

"Now, now, settle down, both of you!" He said calmly, as if we were still foals. "I'm sure we can find a way to settle this, other than challenging one another."

"We're not foals anymore, dad! We're almost 2 years old! We're teenagers! We can handle this ourselves, thank you!" Sterling and I were just bringing up our front hooves to pummel each other, when an ear piercing howl split through the air. Everyone froze with fear, and Sterling and I immediately put our hooves back on the ground. I looked over and saw Sterling's eyes wide with fear, his hooves frozen to the spot. Everyone knew to be afraid of that cry. It was the most ferocious wolf in a 100-mile radius. He had tried to fight my dad, and the most powerful horse in the herd was just lucky to stay alive. After that our herd had fled, but came back here because where we had gone, at least five wolf packs had invaded our territory, all working together to drive us out. My dad still had a scar on his face and one really big one across his muscular hindquarters. I looked over at my dad and saw his ears twitching rapidly, and moving this way and that, trying so hard to pinpoint where the sound was coming from. All of a sudden we heard a squeal of terror from the back of the herd, and everyone turned to see Leap, a black and white foal, lifeless. A terrible bite in his neck showed he had been killed by Asher, the fearsome wolf.

"NO!" The scream came from his mother, Josey, a paint mare who had been frozen to the spot like the rest of us, her baby next to her.

"Come out and meet me, you coward, or else I'll just keep picking off members of your so-called herd." The savage growl came from the forest shadows, and all the horses turned towards the voice. I heard the crackling of leaves and cracking of branches as his paws carried him over the forest floor. We soon saw his cold, yellow eyes glinting out of the shadows. My muscles tensed as he showed himself, his muscular body rippling under his smooth, gray fur. His tail was bushy, and I caught a glimpse of his deadly sharp teeth as he curled his lips back in a snarl. I felt my dad pushing through the fearful bodies as he made his way to where Asher was standing. I quickly glimpsed at my dad and saw no fear in his eyes. His muscles were rippling under his skin, and he held his head up proud. I tried to detect any fear-scent that might be coming from him, but it was hard. I couldn't pick out his scent above all of the others'

fear-scents. As my dad approached Asher, he put his ears back and prepared for battle. Asher got low to the ground, his ears also pinned back and his lips pulled back, revealing his teeth. My dad stopped a few feet in front of the deadly wolf.

"I thought I might go hunting, but then when I realized this was your herd, I decided to just come and end this once and for all. I will win," The traitorous wolf growled through bared teeth.

"You have already killed one of this herd. Isn't that enough?" "NEVER!!" The wolf replied.

"I would have rather taken the place of Leap, but you had to kill an innocent little foal. If I killed you right now, I would at least have a reason! You have killed many animals, and I would be getting revenge for their families and friends. You just kill for fun. For the so-called satisfaction of it!"

"Not true! I kill to eat, to survive, not for the fun of it! And it's time I get a nice, big meal out of you!!" And with that, he sprung. My dad reared up as Asher landed on top of his back, trying to grab hold of him. Asher went flying through the air, but just managed to land on his feet. My dad reared up at him as Asher sprung again, but Asher dove down and slashed my dad's chest, then slid out from under him and slunk into the bushes. My dad's eyes rolled in his head as he tried to find Asher. His chest was slowly dripping blood to the ground. He was panting wildly. I saw a gray bundle of muscle and fur leap onto my dad and latch himself onto his back.

"Get OFF!" My dad yelled furiously as he reared and bucked to get him off. Asher shifted as my dad landed on the ground, and dug his fangs into his neck. With a shriek, my dad fell to the ground, lifeless. I had watched the whole thing and observed how they fought.

Immediately, I leaped off the ground and smashed Asher to the ground. I was leader now, and it was my duty to protect the herd. Asher yelped with pain as he skidded across the ground and hit his head on a rock. I ran at him again, but Asher was faster than I had expected. He quickly ran behind me, and I felt a sharp pain on my left shoulder as he tried to grasp onto me. I gave a vigorous shake as I reared up, and Asher fell on the ground. I caught a glance of Moon trying to push through the crowd to help me.

"Stay away, Moon! It's too dangerous!" "I want to help!"

"Stay away!" I yelled furiously, as I tried to hold Asher to the ground. He brought up his paw and scratched me on my leg. It was shallow, but the pain was great enough to make me back away. I saw Moon racing at Asher a few feet away from me, and quickly rammed into her, knocking her to the ground.

"Stay away, Moon!" I whinnied a warning at her as she got back up off the ground. I felt a deep gash appear on my back, and quickly thought of an idea. I reared up, and purposely tipped back and collapsed on top of Asher. I heard a terrifying yelp of pain and a crack as I landed. I quickly got back up and looked down to where Asher was struggling to get to his feet. I noticed that his back leg was at a weird angle. That was the snap that I had heard! He finally got to his feet, glared at me, and limped into the woods.

"This isn't finished," I heard him growl bitterly through the trees as I took in what had just happened.

As all the horses crowded around me, praised me, and told me how sorry they were for the loss of my dad, I realized that it was my duty to protect this herd, and make critical decisions about life, which was stressful. However, as I looked around at the horses, I knew what my dad had meant when he had said, "It's the horses that make the land beautiful."

About the Author

Lillian Stielstra lives in Holland, Michigan with her family. She loves spending time at a nearby horse barn riding and caring for the horses and ponies. In her spare time, she reads, hangs out with friends and plays outside. She also loves training her two dogs. Often, she will snuggle with her cat. She loves doing anything outside.

Youth Readers' Choice Winner

Who Knows Where The Railroad Goes
Zack Zupin

A good book for young elementary students.
To Mom and Dad-
I'm trying to get my first book published just for you guys. You guys are
the best parents I could ever wish for. You two are my good luck charms.

-Your son

Over the river, under the snows.

Who knows where the railroad goes?

All over the desert, out in the sun,
Over the river, under the snows,
Who knows where the railroad goes?

Under the archway, through the canyon,
All over the desert, out in the sun,
Over the river, under the snows,
Who knows where the railroad goes?

Next to the village, in the meadow
Under the archway, through the canyon,
All over the desert, out in the sun.
Over the river, under the snows,
Who knows where the railroad goes?

Through the tunnels, way down low,
Next to the village, in the meadow,
Under the archway, through the canyon,
All over the desert, out in the sun,Over the river, under the snows,
Who knows where the railroad goes?

Along the beach, with a good summer breeze,
Through the tunnels, way down low
Next to the village, in the meadow,
Under the archway, through the canyon,

All over the desert, out in the sun,
Over the river, under the snows,
Who knows where the railroad goes?

Under the sun, across the seas,
Along the beach, with a good summer breeze,
Through the tunnels, way down low,
Next to the village, in the meadow,
Under the archway, through the canyon,
All over the desert, out in the sun,
Over the river, under the snows,
Who knows where the railroad goes?

Past the plants, and the dancing monkeys,
Under the sun, across the seas,
Along the beach, with a good summer breeze,
Through the tunnels, way down low,
Next to the village, in the meadow,
Under the archway, through the canyon,
All over the desert, out in the sun,
Over the river, under the snows,
Who knows where the railroad goes?

All through the forests, all through the trees,
Past the plants, and the dancing monkeys,
Under the sun, across the seas,
Along the beach, with a good summer breeze,
Through the tunnels, way down low,
Next to the village, in the meadow,
Under the archway, through the canyon,
All over the desert, out in the sun,
Over the river, under the snows,
Who knows where the railroad goes?

Right by the ghosttown, filled with crooks,
All through the forest, all through the trees,
Past the plants, and the dancing monkeys,
Under the sun, across the seas,
Along the beach, with a good summer breeze,
Through the tunnels, way down low,
Next to the village, in the meadow,

Under the archway, through the canyon,
All over the desert, out in the sun,
Over the river, under the snows,
Who knows where the railroad goes?

Into the forest, filled with peaceful brooks,
Right by the ghosttown, filled with crooks,
All through the forest, all through the trees,
Past the plants, and the dancing monkeys,
Under the sun, across the seas,
Along the beach, with a good summer breeze,
Through the tunnels, way down low,
Next to the town, in the meadow,
Under the archway, through the canyon,
All over the desert, out in the sun,
Over the river, under the snows,
Who knows where the railroad goes?

Past your everyday elephant, and your small-but sly fox,
Into the forest, filled with peaceful brooks,
Right by the ghosttown, filled with crooks,
All through the forest, all through the trees,
Past the plants, and the dancing monkeys,
Under the sun, across the seas,
Along the beach, with a good summer breeze,
Through the tunnels, way down low,
Next to the village, in the meadow,
Under the archway, through the canyon,
All over the desert, out in the sun,
Over the river, under the snows,
Who knows where the railroad goes?

Around the mountains, by the great big rocks,
Past your everyday elephant, and your small-but-sly fox,
Into the forest, full of peaceful brooks,
Right by the ghosttown, filled with crooks,
All through the forest, all through the trees,
Past the plants, and the dancing monkeys,
Under the sun, across the seas,
Along the beach, with a good summer breeze,

Through the tunnels, way down low,
Next to the village, in the meadow,
Under the archway, through the canyon,
All over the desert, out in the sun,
Over the river, under the snows,
Who knows where the railroad goes?

By the castle, where the king holds his crown,
Around the mountain, by the great big rocks,
Past your everyday elephant, and small-but-sly fox,
Into the forest, filled with peaceful brooks,
Right by the ghosttown, filled with crooks,
All through the forest, all through the trees,
Past the plants, and the dancing monkeys,
Under the sun, across the seas,
Along the beach, with a good summer breeze,
Through the tunnels, way down low,
Next to the village, in the meadow,
Under the archway, through the canyon,
All over the desert, out in the sun,
Over the river, under the snows,
Who knows where the railroad goes?

Out in the plains, going through town,
By the castle, where the king holds his crown,
Around the mountains, by the great big rocks,
Past your everyday elephant, and small-but sly-fox,
Into the forest, filled with peaceful brooks,
Right by the ghosttown, filled with crooks,
All through the forest, all through the trees,
Past the plants, and the dancing monkeys,
Under the sun, across the seas,
Along the beach, with a good summer breeze,
Through the tunnels, way down low,
Next to the village, in the meadow,
Under the archway, through the canyon,
All over the desert, out in the sun,
Over the river, under the snows,
Who knows where the railroad goes?

Through the growing city, with the sound of drills,

Out in the plains, going through town,
By the castle, where the king holds his crown,
Around the mountains, by the great big rocks,
Past your everyday elephant, and small-but-sly fox,
Into the forest, filled with peaceful brooks,
Right by the ghosttown, filled with crooks,
All through the forest, all through the trees,
Past the plants, and the dancing monkeys,
Under the sun, across the seas,
Along the beach, with a good summer breeze,
Through the tunnels, way down low, Next to the village, in the meadow,
Under the archway, through the canyon,
All over the desert, out in the sun,
Over the river, under the snows,
Who knows where the railroad goes?

Below the jungle, over the hills,
Through the growing city, with the sound of drills,
Out in the plains, going through town,
By the castle, where the king holds his crown,
Around the mountains, by the great big rocks,
Past your everyday elephant, and small-but-sly fox,
Into the forest, filled with peaceful brooks,
Right by the ghosttown, filled with crooks,
All through the forest, all through the trees,
Past the plants, and the dancing monkeys,
Under the sun, across the seas,
Along the beach, with a good summer breeze,
Through the tunnels, way down low,
Next to the village, in the meadow,
Under the archway, through the canyon,
All over the desert, out in the sun,
Over the river, under the snows,
Who knows where the railroad goes?

To the city, the railroad goes,
Over the river and under the snows.
To the train station, of course it goes there,
It passed some giraffes, two rhinos and a bear.
It dropped off some passengers, who walked with delight,
They finally got dropped off, on this beautiful night.

So be thankful for your trains and cars,
And the NASA spaceship that goes to Mars.
And the airplane flying in the sky blue,
They all transport people just for you.

About the Author

Zack Zupin lives in Michigan. He lives in a suburban home with his family and fish and goes to school like any other kid. In his free time, he likes to either play games or type stories on his computer. Zack dreams of becoming an author and has been writing books since preschool. He has a whole bin of paper-made books that he created.

Youth Published Finalist

Space Cat
Ellie Hardy

Callie the cat had always wanted to go to outer space. She wanted to put on a space suit and float above the earth. Then, one day her chance came.

Callie was at cat school when her teacher, Miss Tuna, said, "Class, in two days there will be a CASA Student Spaceship Trip."

Callie raised her paw. "Can I go?" she asked.

"Sure!" said Miss Tuna. She handed Callie a signing flyer. Callie was the happiest cat in the in universe! But, her parents would have to sign the flyer first.

That evening at dinner Callie told her family the news. Her dad was so surprised that he almost choked on his tunafish.

"So will you sign the flyer?" Callie asked.

"Well, okay," said her dad. "But only on one condition. No space walks." "Okay, I'll start packing!" Callie said. She was so happy!

Callie jittered in her seat as the rocket came into view. The car turned. They parked.

Callie grabbed her bags, said goodbye to her family and walked towards the rocket. She gave a cat with a mustache her flyer. She crawled through the hatch and climbed up to her seat.

"Hmmm," said Callie. "Where can I put my bags?" She found a hook behind her seat and hung up her bags.

She heard a cat's voice. "10, 9, 8, 7, 6, 5, 4, 3, 2, 1, blastoff!"

Callie heard a low, rumbling sound. Then, kaboom! They shot off the ground like a bullet.

Callie gazed in awe at the earth from above. She also studied the moon and its craters. She also tried to get the hang of strapping herself to her bed. She looked at the sunrise and the other planets through a telescope. Callie jumped every time a part of the rocket fell off. Callie was having a great time!

Soon, it was time for lunch. They had tunafish.

Callie did flips and spins until she got very dizzy and had to stop. The trip lasted 3 days. Callie missed her family but she still had fun.

On the last day of the trip, there was a problem. Someone needed to go into the control panel.

Both of the pilots tried to fit in the panel to push the button, but they were too big. One of the pilots turned to Callie."You need to go up there and push it," he said. They helped Callie into the little cubbyhole and she pushed the button!

When she got back to earth, Callie was on the news!

Callie knew she would always remember that amazing trip.

About the Author

Ellie is a third grade girl from Rockford, Michigan. She loves reading, Minecraft®, spelling, writing, science and doing crafts. She lives with her mom, dad and pet fish. Someday Ellie would like to become a writer.

Youth Published Finalist

All for a Placement
Shelley Ouyang

I remembered diving into the pool a few days ago. I remembered how panicked I felt when water rushed into my eyes and I couldn't see. But even though I got last place, I had been racing people who were over my age group. I made the cut half a second earlier than the previous one. But instead of feeling triumphant, I felt nervous and scared all over again, knowing that in a few days I would have to swim again.

"You're definitely going to make a J.O. cut at the swim meet."

My coach said this about three days ago. And guess what? Through dumb luck, I actually did. I had just made a J.O. cut (Junior Olympics) for 100 FR. (100 meters of freestyle) Problem was, we live in Wisconsin. The next meet was more than four hours away.

"Come ON, Mom!" I pleaded. "You know it's a waste of time and money. It's not like I'm going to place or anything. Plus, don't we have to go visit my cousins in Illinois tomorrow?"

"We changed the schedule already. Your cousins can wait until next week. They're really excited about your races, you know. You're supposed to be their role model, right?" Mom didn't even look up from her phone.

"Mooom, Brett's already ten! And Kira's almost nine!"

"Jayden, I've already told your coach that you'll be going. Plus, you really like swimming, don't you? If you're going to join more challenging levels, you might have to travel even more. We have a day until we need to leave. Also, quit whining. It's not going to get you anywhere."

I was shocked. I did love swimming, but not THAT much. I hated going to most swim meets because diving was my worst enemy. Almost every time, I would get my goggles filled up to the brim with water, and have to swim my events "blindfolded." Come on, I said to myself.

The meet's not going to last longer than a day. You'll be fine. Absolutely NOT, the other half of my brain responded.

Seeing how miserable I was, Mom told me that I could put off my math and reading homework for the next two days. But that didn't make me feel much better.

A few days later, I was packing my swim bag. Towels, check. Shoes, check.

Chairs, check. Caps and goggles, check. Markers, check. What else was I missing? I felt like something was off, but I couldn't tell what. But before I had time to go look around, Mom yelled at me to get into the car, so I put my parka on and left the house.

During the trip, I wanted to contact my friends. They didn't swim, but at least it would be good to get some moral support. I fumbled around for my phone -- and guess what? It wasn't there.

Oh CRAP! Without my phone, I couldn't text. Even worse, I wouldn't be able to see my heat and lane beforehand. This wasn't good at all. Everything was falling apart! I asked Mom to see if she had the heats and lanes on her phone, but of course, she didn't. I moaned through the rest of the trip. My brain was too panicked to think straight.

By the time we got to the pool, I was a nervous wreck. We had arrived around half an hour early, but that didn't help much, considering it only took me around five minutes to get my swimsuit on. Following the maps around the building, I found my way to the pool quickly. I was setting my chairs down when I ran into my coach.

"Good to see you here, Jayden!" he grinned. "You ready for your 100 FR?"

"When do the heats and lanes get posted?" I asked, avoiding the question. "They'll get posted when we're ready," he said. "Don't worry, you'll be fine."

I'm not sure if he was trying to use reverse-psychology because worrying was exactly what I was doing.

I spent the first half of the meet sitting in my chair and awaiting my doom. But when they announced my event, I was a jumble of emotions.

Apparently, when the information sheet (or the "heat sheet," as I liked to call it) came out, I had missed it. So I had no idea when I was going to swim or what lane I was. Grabbing my goggles, I ran to the lanes and checked every lane. I had no clue which lane I belonged to, because the timers at each lane were busy with the first heat. Knowing that the fastest people were in lanes three, four, and five, I decided to wait at lane six.

When the first heat finished, I scrambled around, asking anyone who would listen. "Hello! Um, excuse me, but -- oh, nevermind.Um, hi! Do you know which lane I -- forget about it."

But when the swimmers stepped up onto the diving blocks, I saw an empty space. That's probably my lane! I rushed to lane four, putting my goggles on. "Oh, hi! Are you Jayden?" asked the timer.

I nodded, and got on the block just in time. "Take your mark." We were starting! I took a deep breath. It'll be over in a moment.

BEEP!!! The horn sounded, and we all dove in.

Instantly, water filled my goggles around halfway. But that wasn't what worried me. I felt an aching cramp in my side. Due to not warming up before I raced, my body decided that it would be a good idea to give me a cramp. NOT NOW! I reached the surface of the water, gritted my teeth, and swam for my life.

The pool was fifty meters long, and I only needed to swim one lap. At the other end of the pool, during the flipturn, I was the only one at the wall. Oh no, I thought. I swam the wrong event, didn't I? Augh, I guess I'll just get disqualified. What did I expect? First place? While I was distracted, I missed the wall and only pushed off with my toes. It pulled my cramp and sent a wave of pain throughout me. But at this point, I was already too panicked to think anymore.

I reached the wall, panting and gasping for breath. I fully expected someone to yell at me to get out and swim the next heat, but nobody did. I was very confused, and turned to the scoreboard. What I saw shocked me.

Nitro, Jayden   Lane 4 1st

I rubbed my eyes and looked again. Yes, it was still there.

But that's not possible! First place?

Me?

WHAT?

"Swimmers, exit the pool." I climbed out of the pool, and was greeted by the timer, who was holding a ribbon. "Great job!" she exclaimed with a smile.

The rest of the meet felt like a dream, mainly because that was my only event. When I got back into the car to go home, I relaxed and grinned.

Maybe swim meets aren't that bad.

End.

About the Author

Shelley Ouyang is a sixth grader at Slauson Middle School. She enjoys writing fantasy stories, and lives with her parents. She plays piano and violin, participates in her swim team, and loves to ski and snowboard occasionally.

Youth Published Finalist

The Stones
Andrew Wright

One rather dreary day James was collecting rocks, his usual daily activity, when his shovel hit something. He looked but did not see what he expected. This stone was the most beautiful thing he had ever dug out of the ground! He was amazed! How did it glow like that? He gently brought it out of the ground. He looked into it, and what he saw scared him to death.

§

Michael was terrified, the noble wolf kingdom had been talking about an attack for weeks. He imagined it would be a small band of rebels who would be convinced to leave in a few waves of combat. But this was much worse than he could have imagined. His father's soldiers were falling faster than he could count. It was an awful scene. The rebels were fighting towards the gate; they had a battering ram. The gate shook, becoming weaker and weaker with each blow. The last of his father's soldiers braced the gate. Finally, the suspense was broken, the rebels broke through the gate. They poured through the gate, killing the rest of the soldiers.

Michael couldn't believe this was happening. His bodyguard, and friend, had locked himself and Michael in his room as a precaution. Michael had seen all the events from the window. Suddenly they heard the rebels pounding on the door.

"Go through the trapdoor," Michael's bodyguard whispered. His bodyguard moved the chair and the mat and opened the trapdoor. Michael went through, and he closed the trapdoor behind him. He heard his friend move the chair and the mat back, then he heard splintering wood. The rebels had broken through! He heard snarls, swords clashing, and a howl of pain.

Michael knew that howl.

"No" Michael whimpered. He kept saying the same thing over and over as he went down the spiraling staircase and through the dark corridor."No, no, no, no." He stopped at a door. He collected himself, opened the door, and ran.

§

James saw all that Michael saw through the stone! He saw vicious wolves attacking each other, he saw them break through the gate, and he saw Michael running down the staircase and through the corridor. James was astonished. He had never seen anything like this. Suddenly the scene blurred. He was confused.

His mother came out of the house; he panicked. He stuffed the stone in his jacket. "Come inside it's time for supper," his mother called. James grabbed his bucket and shovel, ran to the door, and went inside.

He sat down at the table; his father blessed the food, and they started to eat. When they were done he went into his room and locked the door. He pulled out the stone and looked into it.

§

Michael ran faster than he had ever needed to before. It was a short distance from the door to the forest, but he didn't want to be seen. He closed in on the forest in a matter of seconds. He reached the forest, but he did not stop. He ran hard into the forest. He ran on and on until he finally collapsed on the ground with exhaustion. He clung to his satchel to see if the precious stone was there. Michael pulled it out. The stone had always been a mystery. The stone had been passed down from the royal family for generations. The treasure had seemed to glow, but when he looked deeply into the stone it darkened. That was why he was so surprised when he looked into it and saw a creature he'd never seen or heard of before.

"What are you?" Michael said without the slightest inclination of what a human was.

"What do you mean what am I? I'm a person, a human. Oh, and you can talk?" said James, completely baffled by the whole ordeal.

"Of course I can talk. And what do you mean, hu...man? And how am I talking to you, and how are you talking to me? And where are you?" said Michael.

This conversation went on for quite a long time, from one question to another, with precious few answers. The questions finally died down, and they got down to some answers. They decided to tell all about themselves so that there would be no need for questions. They also decided for Michael to start first.

"Well," said Michael, "I am the son of the king, Michael Wolfband the ninth. I will be the tenth king. I may already be. My father went away to arrange a peace treaty with a neighboring kingdom. I'm starting to think that the rebels that attacked my father's kingdom were not rebels at all but possibly the kingdom that my father tried to make peace with. If true, I suppose that the negotiations for peace have failed, and my father was captured or..."

"Killed?" said James, not able to even imagine how Michael felt.

"Yes, I need to think and find out what I'm going to do; so, goodbye for now," Michael said as if a heavy load had been lifted onto his shoulders.

"Michael!" James shouted, but it was too late. The stone went black.

§

After thinking for a long time Michael remembered that his father had given him a map. His father said that if something ever went wrong, he was alone, and there seemed to be no hope, to get the stone and find his sword. Then he should follow the map his father had given him and run to the Ancient Mountains indicated on the map. So Michael did what his father had instructed except for finding his father's sword, but he didn't think it would make much of a difference. So he ran with all the strength he had only stopping to look at the map, eat, and rest.

Finally, after a fortnight of trying to race to the Ancient Mountains and survive at the same time, he saw the top of the colossal mountains he had tried so hard to get to. He ran toward the mountains with renewed vigor. Once he reached the first mountain he saw the enormous mouth of a cave. The cave's mouth was shaped like a creature that he had only heard and read about, a dragon. It looked almost sad and yet fearsome at the same time. He thought that it might be the light of the moon, for it was always night in that world. He walked into the mouth of the cave. The instant he walked in, he heard a deep, scratchy voice.

"I am the king of the Dragon Horde. Who enters the dragon's dwelling?" said the dragon without any rise or fall of his voice.

"I am Michael Wolfband the tenth. My father told me to come to this place whenever the kingdom and myself were in dire need," Michael said rather shakily.

"Only the one who possesses the stone and the sword may command the Dragon Horde," said the dragon king.

"I have the stone," Michael said, pulling out the gem. "But I don't have the sword." "Then leave," the dragon said. Michael hesitated. "Leave!" he said with such a terrifying growl that Michael bolted out of the cave. As he was running away from the dragon cave mouth, he looked back at it. He was not being followed. He slowed to a stop and looked at the map. He looked at the map and found the kingdom his father went to, "The Brother Clan." The reason it was called that was because it was ruled by three brothers called, "The Three." He pulled his compass and found the direction he would go.

After he took a nap, he ran toward The Brother Clan. After another week of running, he saw the city with a thick wall around it; but before he got to the clearing, he saw a cabin. He slowly jogged up to the door and knocked.

"Is anyone in there?" he said, out of breath. The door swung open and hit Michael on the side of his head, everything went black.

§

Michael woke to the sound of a brass pipe. The sound was shrill, and the notes flowed smoothly. When he opened his eyes he saw an old wolf; he was the one who was playing the pipe. The old wolf's fingers nimbly covered hole after hole in the pipe; the pattern created a cheerful melody.

"Who are you?" Michael said.

"Ah, you're awake. Oh, and my name is Finneon. And, yours?" said the old wolf apparently named Finneon.

"Where am I?" Michael said, trying to direct the conversation away from who he was. "Ahh, just like your father, trying to point the conversation away from who you are," said Finneon.

Michael shot out of bed. "My father! How do you know about my father? Where is he?" Michael said, hopeful that his father might still be alive.

"Ooh, your father, your father is dead," said Finneon with a sudden sadness washing over him.

"No, no!" Michael said, then ran out of the cabin, scampered up a tree, and there he wept with great sorrow.

§

Michael wept all day and all night; in the morning he noticed he was hungry. So he went into the cabin to see if he could find some food.

"Are you ready for some breakfast?" said Finneon cheerfully. "Uh, yes, thank you," Michael said with some hesitation.

"Then eat, come eat," he said. Finneon sat him down in a chair at a small table. Michael ate like it was the first time he had eaten in months. After he had eaten he talked with Finneon.

"Before you speak you must hear me out," Finneon said. "Your father escaped imprisonment in the dungeon of The Three, he even managed to get back his sword, but he did not escape without a price. When he was running across the clearing around the castle, a sentinel pierced him with an arrow in the back. But I was there, and I shot the sentinel before he could sound the alarm. I ran to your father and dragged him to my cabin. I was amazed that he survived long enough to tell me what he did,"

"What did he tell you? When did this happen?" Michael said, a bit afraid of what the answers would be.

"It happened three days ago. He told me to go on a journey to find his son, you, and when he was found to give him the sword of his father. With that said, he breathed his last," Finneon said.

"Do you have the sword?" Michael said.

"Yes, I do. I meant to leave to find you, but you came to me. Uh, here it is," Finneon said, pulling out an ornately fashioned sword out of a chest. He gave it to Michael.

"It is beautiful, but wait, there is an indentation in the pommel of the sword. Oh, is it for the stone?" said Michael very much intrigued.

"Stone, what stone?" said Finneon.

Michael pulled out the stone and said, "This stone."

"The dragon's egg! Then that must be the dragon's claw!" Finneon said full of wonder. "Huh, what do you mean, dragon's egg, dragon's claw?" Michael said.

"Those were the original names for them. The sword was forged by the dragon's own hands and their own fiery breath. The stone was found by the dragons in the heart of the mountain they lived in. You see the objects weren't really what they were called. And the legend says that if the stone is put in its right place, in the pommel of the sword, the person who possesses the sword and stone together will become almost indestructible. That person will have the might and power of a dragon, and only the one who places the stone in its place could ever take it out," Finneon said.

"I will have the might and power of a dragon?" Michael asked, amazed.

"There's one way to test the ancient legend; put the stone into its rightful place," Finneon said with determination. Michael slowly moved the stone toward the pommel. Finally the stone and the pommel of the sword touched. Immediately the sword burst into flame. Suddenly the faintness he was feeling was gone. In place of it, he felt a strength beyond anything he had ever imagined, a strength beyond the race of wolves, the strength of a dragon.

§

After a few more hours of talking to Finneon, Michael ran with the strength of a dragon to the Ancient Mountains. It took him a week to get to Finneon's house, but it took him one day to get back to the dragon's cave. Once there, he walked straight up to the cave without hesitation. Once he was in the cave he was the one who spoke first.

"I am Michael Wolfband the tenth, and I have the stone and the sword. I command you to follow me in battle against The Brother Clan," he said defiantly.

"Show us the blade and the stone, and you have our allegiance," said the dragon king.

With that said, he drew the ancient fiery blade, with the stone embedded in the pommel. "You have the allegiance of Cynrad the king of the Dragon Horde, and here is your army." Suddenly, the cave was illuminated by a blast of dragon breath. There were thousands of dragons, organized, with centurions, crowned with a helmet that was made of a metal Michael had never seen. The fire the dragons breathed was to light torches lined on the sides of the cave. Cynrad spoke, "Where is the place of battle?"

§

Next thing Michael knew, he was on the back of Cynrad flying through mid air. Flying! This was the battle strategy: fly above the clouds and then when they were above the Kingdom of Wolfband, Cynrad and Michael would dive down to the city. Cynrad would let Michael down, and then Cynrad would fly back above the clouds. The army would circle in the air around the city until Michael gave the signal. Then the army would fly down upon the city and drive out The Three from his father's former kingdom.

They were almost there now. Finally, they were above the city where Michael's real nightmare had begun. Cynrad dived with Michael on his back. When they landed, Cynrad dropped Michael off and flew back up quickly and quietly to go undetected. Michael slipped in and out of the night shadows that were always there in that world. Michael crept closer and closer to the throne room. Finally, he saw the double doors to the throne room. There were two guards, but he could deal with them easily enough. He walked up to the guards and got their attention. Then he ran around the corner; the guards were following him, good. Once he was around the corner, he jumped up and dug his claws into the wall so that he stuck. The guards ran past him. He jumped down from the wall and ran through the double doors.

"By what authority and business do you come bursting in here for," said the eldest of The Three.

"By the authority of myself, Michael Wolfband the tenth, and my business is your surrender. There is an army of dragons waiting for my signal. When they see it they will take the city by force," he said with confidence.

"Pah, dragons are a legend, and I will not lay down my kingdom to some wolf who thinks he can come in here and make me surrender by empty threats," the "ruler" said.

"Very well, that is all I need to know," Michael said. Then he ran at the throne in the middle of the room and jumped up. He landed his kick on the top of the throne, just above the "king's" head and rebounded off the throne so that it would topple backwards. When he landed, he ran out of the throne room while the guards helped the "king". When he was out he ran to a watch tower and ran up the stairs. Once he was at the top he gave the signal, waving the flaming sword in the air.

The Dragon Horde rained down on the city, but when the people saw them they ran out of the city in fear. The city was evacuated in a few minutes. Even the eldest of The Three and his guards ran.

The kingdom was finally restored, but there were no wolves to live in it; or were there? It gave Michael an idea. The prison! Michael went down to the prison and freed the prisoners.

Others, who had escaped into the woods a few weeks ago, saw what had happened and came rushing in, replacing the ones who had run out in fear. The whole kingdom was invited to a feast, but before the feast Michael went into a private room and pulled out the stone.

§

"Michael! I saw all that you did through the stone, again," James said.

"That's great! But I learned that I can journey to your world," Michael said. "That's wonderful, we can meet in person," James said, excited.

"But I cannot, I have to stay here and oversee my kingdom," he said. "But, ...I understand, then, I guess this is...goodbye," said James.

Then they said in unison, "Goodbye." The stones turned black and crumbled to dust. And they began to wonder if those were the only stones of their kind in their Worlds.

The End.

About the Author

Andrew was born in South Carolina and spent the first four years of his life in Cameroon, West Africa. His family moved to Michigan when he was 8 years old. He has two brothers and one sister. He enjoys being outside, making things, and reading. Andrew also likes music and playing the piano.

Spanish Language - Youth Judges' Choice Winner

La Posición
Xavier Irizarry

¡Hola, soy Arc! Me considero inteligente y educado, pero a veces me meto en problemas. Mis amigos dicen que tengo el mejor cabello de todos los niños de la escuela, soy el más alto de mi clase y siempre llevo buena ropa. Pero este año aprendí, que nada de eso importa. Déjame explicarte.

Todo empezó una noche cuando mamá y yo vimos un anuncio de un equipo de fútbol con jugadores mayores que yo. El anuncio decía que buscaban jugadores para completar su equipo. Mi mamá llamó al entrenador, que se llamaba Leonardo De Gea, quien le preguntó: - ¿Arc puede venir a jugar con nosotros?

- Claro que sí -dijo ella- pero, me gustaría saber si podrá seguir jugando en la posición de portero- indagó mi mamá. Después de la conversación mi mamá me explicó que el equipo solamente tenía a un portero y que les hacía falta uno más. Me sentí emocionado, pero esa emoción no duraría mucho.

Pasaron tres semanas hasta la primera práctica. En ella me fue bien porque era el único portero, pero en la segunda práctica me sorprendió ver a dos porteros en el campo que no habían estado presentes en la práctica inicial. Conmigo ya éramos tres porteros en un solo equipo, lo cual no es nada normal, ya que reduce las oportunidades de ser portero en juegos futuros. Entendí que iba a necesitar luchar por la posición de portero principal del equipo. Hubo algunas prácticas en las cuales el entrenador me dijo que jugaría en la portería, pero mis compañeros no tenían fe en mí todavía.- ¡Eres el peor portero que he visto! -me gritó Benjamin cuando una bola me pasó y entró a la portería durante la práctica.

- ¡Ese Arc no puede parar la pelota aunque una tortuga la pateara! – escuché que le susurraba Hudson a John mientras esperábamos en fila para patear.

Me sentí enojado y triste porque lo que decían no era verdad. En casa, se lo conté a mi mamá y ella, enfurecida y molesta, se levantó de su asiento decidida a mandarle un mensaje al entrenador. Pero le pedí que no lo hiciera porque quería ganarme el respeto solo y demostrar que sí puedo ser un buen portero.

Cuando fuimos al primer juego no jugué en la posición de portero. Los otros dos porteros ocuparon la posición, lo cual no me gustó para nada. Jugué como defensa y como delantero. Fue bueno, pero me hubiera encantado poder jugar como portero. En mi mente, pensaba que era raro que no me dieran ninguna oportunidad y lo veía como injusto. Sin embargo, al mismo tiempo, entendí ya que ellos eran mayores que yo.

Cuando fui a la próxima práctica jugué en posición y le enseñé al entrenador lo que podía hacer. Cuando llamó a los otros niños yo le pregunté si podría ir con ellos para jugar en la portería y él contestó -Dale-.

Hice mi mejor esfuerzo y también tuve algunas buenas atajadas. Cuando regresé a casa, después de bañarme me puse a mirar televisión. Durante ese tiempo algo se me vino a la mente. Pensaba que yo tenía todo lo necesario para ser portero y no podía creer que el entrenador De Gea no me hubiera puesto como portero en el primer partido. También pensaba en todo lo demás que mis amigos me dicen, sobre el cabello, ser el más alto y lo de la ropa. Sin embargo, en ese momento podía ver claramente que lo que hay en tu interior es más importante que lo que hay en tu exterior.

En el próximo partido jugué en la cancha, y cuando el silbato sonó para indicar el final de la primera mitad, fue claro que el entrenador no me iba a poner como portero.

- ¿Por qué no dejas que Arc muestre lo que él tiene? -dijo un jugador del equipo.

- ¡Sí! ¡Por favor De Gea! ¡Ponme como portero! Cree en mí –le rogué yo-.

Para mi sorpresa, él dijo que sí. Jugamos todo el partido y cuando llegó el último tiro, la pelota se dirigió hacia mí y yo la detuve, pero al hacerlo me caí y me torcí la muñeca. Cuando me levanté y le dije al entrenador que no podía jugar más porque el dolor era mucho.

Mi mamá me llevó al hospital y mientras esperábamos le pregunté quien había ganado el partido. Ella me dijo que nosotros, lo cual hizo que el dolor se fuera un poco. Lo único que me preocupaba ahora era si el entrenador me dejaría ser portero otra vez. El doctor nos llamó para entrar a su consultorio y examinar mi brazo. Durante la espera noté que había una maquinita y una venda. – ¿Me va a doler? le pregunté a mi mamá - ¿Y para qué la venda médica? - Ella me contestó que la venda servía para ayudar cuando hay torceduras y que se demora tres semanas en sanar.

El doctor me tomó la mano y la puso dentro de la maquinita. Me dijo que tenía una torcedura de muñeca lo cual me espantó y le respondí pesado- ¡Eso es imposible! Es usted un mentiroso ¿Qué está pensando? -le dije al doctor. Mi mamá me gritó:

- ¡ARC CUANDO LLEGUEMOS A CASA TE VAS A IR A TU CAMA Y TE QUEDARÁS AHÍ HASTA LA CENA!

De regreso a casa no hablamos. Yo solo podía pensar en no poder jugar al fútbol por tres semanas lo cual me hizo sentir mal del estómago. Llegamos a casa y me fui directamente al cuarto. Estaba tan enojado que tiré la puerta tan fuerte que probablemente los vecinos lo escucharon. Cuando llegó el tiempo de la cena salí de mi cuarto enojado con mi mamá. Cuando me senté no hablé con ella por los primeros minutos hasta que ella rompió el silencio- Perdón por gritarte en la oficina del doctor -me dijo.

- Perdón por hacer una morisqueta donde el doctor- le dije yo.
- Si quieres puedes ir a las prácticas de fútbol- continuó ella.
- Ok- dije yo arrepentido.

Así que empecé a ir a las prácticas solo a mirar. Dos semanas más tarde fui a uno de nuestros juegos. No pude jugar pero me alegré porque ganamos. Después de ver lo bien que lo hicieron nuestros dos porteros en ese juego, empecé a cuestionar si iba a poder jugar en la portería otra vez. Desde el público podía apreciar lo buenos que ellos eran.

Mi mamá trataba de animarme, insistiendo que el entrenador me daría una oportunidad cuando volviera. Al día siguiente durante una práctica, le enseñé al entrenador que todavía podía jugar con una muñeca torcida. Entrené tanto que cuando llegué a la casa sentía que mis piernas estaban a punto de partirse, pero eso no me iba a detener para seguir trabajando aún más duro.

Cuando me senté en el sofá empecé a pensar sobre lo que mis padres siempre dicen: que los atletas nunca se hacen solo con el talento con el que nacen, sino que practican y practican para mejorar hasta que graban en su mente lo que necesitan saber. Ellos nunca dejan que su cabello, su actitud o su ropa hablen por ellos, sino que ellos hablan por sí mismos con sus acciones. Ahora entiendo por qué siempre están entrenando, que lo hacen para divertirse y para continuar mejorando. Allí sentado, yo sabía que pronto me quitarían la venda y que seguramente podría jugar en el próximo partido.

Llegó el día del partido y en la segunda mitad del juego, me sorprendió que el entrenador me puso en la portería. Le di todo a mi equipo e hice mi mayor esfuerzo, evitando a toda costa que algo entrara en la red, ayudando a ganar el partido.

Ahora, mi equipo me respeta. Eso era lo que yo realmente quería. Soy el portero que va a la cancha para jugar la primera mitad. He aprendido que nunca te van a dar algo gratis y que toma esfuerzo, tiempo y disciplina para poder ganar el respeto de tus amigos. La posición no se gana solamente en la cancha, también se gana en la vida y es una forma de pensar.

About the Author

Xavier Irizarry is a fifth grader who loves sports. He wrote his story about soccer and goalkeeping because he has had his own experiences trying to prove himself on the field. He is most grateful for his family, especially his younger brother Iván, and his friends. Xavier appreciates his teachers at Zeeland Christian School and ZCS global for so much great learning.

Spanish Language - Youth Judges' Choice Runner-Up

Toby y Stanley: Unos perros extraordinarios
Lucio Gunckel

Había una vez en 1976, un perro, Golden Retriever (para ser específico), que nació en San Francisco, California. Se llamaba Stanley, era un perro muy pequeño, con pelo castaño claro y quería hacer muchas cosas porque en esa etapa de su vida no sabía mucho.

Cinco años después, la última cosa de la que tenía memoria era estar corriendo por su vida. Corría en medio del aguacero aunque le tenía miedo a la lluvia. Su mamá, mientras tanto, no sabía a dónde se había ido su hijo.

Unos días después, Stanley fue atrapado por el rescatador de perros, un hombre muy grande con un peluquín rubio, quien lo mandó a la perrera. Estuvo encerado por días, semanas, meses y años, siempre intentando escapar.

Y un buen día por fin se escapó. Para resumir, voy a decir nada más un par de cosas: a media noche excavó un hoyo en el fondo de su jaula, se arrastró debajo de una cerca y saltó hacia un tren que estaba pasando. Cuando por fin estaba en el tren se dijo -¡Esto es supercalifragilisticoespialidoso! Sí, es una palabra muy larga, pero es una palabra que usaba cuando estaba emocionado.

Y entonces se fue a un lugar con mucha basura. Y ahí es donde Stanley se quedó a vivir por el resto de su vida. Tenía toda la comida que quería, pero nunca volvió a ver a su mamá.

§

Vamos al año 2015 con un perro que se llama Toby. Sí, no es nada más que un nombre de cuatro letras, pe(r)ro es un nombre. (¿Notó lo que hice con esa palabra perro/pero)

Ahora regresemos a la historia.

En 2015, Toby, estaba en la perrera también, después de casi ser aplastado como panqueque por un camión de basura. Y si estás pensando que NO SABE nada de su tatara tatara abuelo Stanley, tienes razón. Toby era un Beagle y no un golden retriever porque su mamá era una beagle.

La mayor parte de su vida, Toby fue un perro callejero y comía todo lo que podía. Pero allí no concluye su historia. Un día, estaba intentando encontrar su desayuno en la basura cuando un camión de basura le pasó a menos de un pie de distancia, pero como era perro callejero por gran parte de su vida, sabia como escaparse de muchas eee... "cosas." Así que esta vez escapó de la cosa que a todos los perros tienen les da terror. Pero Toby era mucho más temeroso que los otros perros.

Toby sabía que debía escapar de la perrera. Estaba caminando cuando vio una hoja de papel en la pared con una lista de perros y gatos que nunca fueron encontrados. Uno de los perros anunciados era alguien llamado Stanley. Esa hoja registraba los miembros de todas las familias perrunas. Allí decía que el perro más joven descendiente de la familia de Stanley era un perro que se llama Toby y que tenía cinco años.

Toby pensó -yo tengo cinco años y mi nombre es TOBY ¡Cha cha cha chaaan!

En su mente Toby se está preguntaba-¿Seré yo? Seguro es un perro diferente, ¿verdad? La hoja de papel también detallaba cómo Stanley había escapado muchos anos atrás. Cuando estaba a punto de leer cómo había escapado su antecesor, el dueño de la perrera entró al cuarto y dijo -¡Es hora de cenar!. Toby pensó -voy a esperar hasta mañana para leer eso, pero dos segundos después dijo -¡No! y corrió hacia la hoja de papel saltando. Pero como era bajito, solo logró brincar como a un pie de distancia del piso -¿Por qué tendré las patas tan cortas? ¡Apenas ayer estuvimos practicando parkour no estaban tan mal!

Pero por buena suerte, estaba lo suficientemente cerca para leer cómo su tatatatarabuelo había escapado por el agujero que había excavado. Toby corrió hacia la tapa que estaba encima del hoyo pensando –ya decía yo que esa tapa se veía extraña- pero antes de escapar, se detuvo a comer. Claro que quería ser libre pero también quería comer.

Después de comer corrió hacía el hoyo pero descubrió que estaba obstruido. Toby no podía excavar el agujero porque los beagles son chiquitos y no pueden excavar muy bien. Estaba tan decepcionado porque en ese momento supo que no hay nadie en el mundo que puede excavar como un golden retriever.

Después de meses algo extraño sucedió. Toby fue adoptado por una familia que tenía cuatro humanos. Uno se llama Jack y tenía nueve años, la otra se llama Stacy y también tenía nueve años y sus padres. Mientras los humanos observaban a todos los animales de la perrera, el papá se detuvo y le dijo al dueño - Yo quiero a ese perro.

- Okay –contestó el dueño. Luego se dirigió a Toby y le dijo –has tenido una larga jornada, amigo.

Pero Toby pensó en su mente -No es cierto. Tú y yo no somos amigos.

Una vez fuera de la perrera, Toby miró hacia arriba y vio una cosa gigante y con ruedas. Se veía como un camión de basura al que él no se subiría por nada el mundo. Pero el papá lo quería subir, así que pelearon y lucharon. Toby se aseguró que el papá supiera que el NO QUERÍA SUBIRSE AL CAMIÓN. Como dije antes, Toby es muy temeroso y mientras intentaba resistirse, parecía como si estuviera excavando y era chistoso porque él no había nada que excavar.

Pero el papá tenía un poder secreto: el poder de las cosquillas. Y antes de que Toby se diera cuenta, el papá lo había subido y al camión. Una vez allí, el camión no era tan espantoso como Toby se lo había imaginado.

Durante el viaje a la casa tomó una larga siesta. Cuando llegaron a la casa, se desmayó y la última cosa que vio fue un conejo bien rechoncho. Cuando recuperó la conciencia estaba muy enojado pero no sabía por qué. Después se acordó que había un conejo que lo había hecho desmayar. Y desde ese momento Toby le declaró la guerra al conejo rechoncho.

Toby escribió una carta al conejo que decía - Ruff ruff, bark ruff, ruff bark ruff ruff. La traducción es "nos vemos en el patio trasero a las cinco en punto. Y Toby fue a explorar la casa hasta las cinco. Revisó todos los cuartos y declaró que todos le pertenecían a él. Pero después de cinco minutos sabía que no podía hacer eso porque los niños lo echaron de sus recámaras.

Cuando llegaron las cinco, Toby fue al patio trasero y cayó en una trampa hecha por el conejo justo antes de salir de la puerta. Se trataba de una trampa estilo Bugs Bunny con un lazo que se cierra cuando la pisas. Cuando por fin salió de la trampa, vio al conejo, quien le dijo -Estoy listo. Y si estás pensando que no se estaban peleando, estás equivocado. Estaban peleando con sus juguetes pero se veía como si estuvieran jugando. Estaban diciendo cosas como "yo voy a ganar" y "no, definitivamente soy you el que voy a ganar".

Entonces los dos vieron los juguetes que tenían y dijeron al mismo tiempo - ¿A ti también te gusta el gato Tom?"

Toby dijo -Sí ¿Has de pensar que a mi me gusta Jerry el ratoncito, no?

Y los dos sonrieron y se fueron a la casa felices.

Cuando Jack les preguntó a los dos -¿Qué le pasó a los juguetes? Toby le respondió en el lenguaje de los perros -casi nada.

Y así fue como Toby llegó a ser feliz con su nueva familia y su amigo rechoncho.

El Fin.

About the Author

Lucio Gunckel was born in Los Angeles, California and currently resides in Ann Arbor, Michigan. He likes drawing, doing parkour, and drumming. He's a third grader at Allen Elementary. He enjoys traveling to Oaxaca to eat huevos al comal and to hang out with relatives.

Spanish Language - Youth Readers' Choice Winner

¡La espía Catalina!
Cailynn Hamilton

En medio de la noche, cuando solo se podía ver la luna, Catalina estaba persiguiendo a Sila por haberse robado su diamante bañado en oro puro. Este artefacto era muy especial para Catalina porque había sido un regalo de su madre. Catalina persiguió a Sila por las montañas de Oruga, los cañones Mariposa y la calle de la Merienda, donde Sila se robaba comida.

- ¡Catalina! - exclamó Sila cuando la vio acercándose a ella.

- Hoy no te me vas a escapar -susurró Catalina.

Después de una hora de persecución, Catalina había capturado a Sila y la entregó a la policía, pero Sila, que era más inteligente que la policía, se escapó.

- Catalina no se imagina lo que voy a hacer -susurró Sila, quien tenía un plan tan malvado que nadie podría arruinarlo, según ella.

En la mañana, cuando Catalina se despertó, se enteró del escape de Sila y fue directamente a su casa. ¡Vaya la sorpresa que se llevó! Sila había escapado de la cárcel, pero ¿Qué más estará tramando ahora? –se preguntaba Catalina. Encontró pistas de dibujos de una corona y de la reina. Pensó y pensó hasta que todo le hizo sentido: Sila estaba tratando de robarse la corona de la reina.

De repente ¡Bam! Sila entró a su casa mientras exclamaba - ¡Hoy es el día!

- ¡Oh no! – pensó Catalina mientras se escondía en un rincón- ahora todo tiene sentido, Sila estaba diciendo "hoy es el día" porque era el día del baile de la reina . ¡SE VA A ROBAR LA CORONA HOY! ¿Qué debo hacer? -pensó Catalina- ¡voy a ir a ese baile! –pensó decidida.

Cuando Catalina llegó al baile fue directamente donde se encontraba la reina para protegerla, pero ¡LA CORONA YA NO ESTABA!

- ¿Será que Sila llegó primero? – se preguntó Catalina-.

¡BOOM!

¡Yo conozco ese boom! -pensó Catalina- era Sila.

- Hola a todos, tengo una sorpresa muy especial para la reina -dijo Sila- pero antes de que pudiera hacer nada...

- ¡Boom!

- ¿Qué fue eso? -Pensó Catalina- Era la policía y los guardias de la reina quienes capturaron a Sila y se la llevaron a la cárcel. Desde ese día Catalina siempre se pregunta: ¿Será que debo convertirme en policía? Catalina fue a la estación policial y susurró -Gracias- pero antes de que la policía pudiera ver quién había dicho "gracias", Catalina desapareció.

§

Cuando Catalina despertó, vio que seguía siendo una niña pero que había tenido un sueño lleno de aventuras y quiso contárselo a toda su clase. Pero al hacerlo, todos pensaron que no era sino una broma. Después de eso, nadie quería jugar con Catalina durante el recreo, pero a ella no le importaba, por más que los niños se portaban groseros con ella. Decidió no contarle a su mamá lo que le estaba pasando porque pensaba que su mamá no la dejaría jugar si se enteraba de que habia niños molestándola.

El siguiente sábado, Catalina y su mejor amiga Rosa fueron al parque de Mary Worth. Ese día, la mamá de Rosa le dejo saber a la mamá de Catalina que había niños molestándola en la escuela.

La mamá de Catalina estaba muy sorprendida mientras caminaba hacia donde se columpiaba Catalina - ¿Por qué no me hablaste sobre los niños que te molestan?- le preguntó.

Catalina le respondió que no quería que ella se enterara porque... - porque no quería que fueras a la escuela. Me sentiría humillada -confesó Catalina.

- Yo nunca te humillaría ni te haría pasar vergüenza –le contestó su madre.

Después de algunos días las dos niñas, Catalina y Rosa, y las dos madres, la mamá de Catalina y la mamá de Rosa, llevaron a toda la clase de Catalina a la heladería donde los niños compartieron todos juntos. Fue desde aquel día que Catalina no ha tenido nadie que la moleste sobre sus sueños que se convierten en cuentos como este, porque ahora, a todo el mundo le encanta escuchar las historias de la autora CATALINA SALINA.

Entonces, si tú tienes tiempo en tu vida para leer un de sus libros, no pases por alto esa oportunidad.

About the Author

Cailynn was born in Grand Rapids, MI. She began her Spanish Immersion Education at age 3, and has developed a love for reading and writing in both Spanish and English. She has written many stories. Cailynn is an energetic and creative entrepreneur. She has a jewelry making business and is currently producing a kids cooking show for YouTube. Cailynn also enjoys recreational swimming, gymnastics, crafts, music, traveling with her family and learning about different cultures.

Spanish Language - Youth Published Finalist

El Sr. José
Harper Davis

Un día, el Sr. Márquez les dijo a sus estudiantes de cuarto grado que los hechiceros y las hechiceras eran reales -Los hechiceros pueden hacer muchas cosas, como mover objetos con varitas mágicas y transformar personas en animales u objetos. Pero solamente los hechiceros y hechiceras malos usan la magia para el mal.

Les contó de un lugar no muy lejano, que en realidad puede ser donde sea, pero solo las personas que conocen de magia saben llegar, incluyendo muchos hechiceros muy mágicos. Uno de los hechiceros en ese lugar se llamaba José. Él podía hacer mucho más que otros hechiceros.

Un buen día cuando los hechiceros se encontraban reunidos, incluyendo algunos muy chicos, algo no estaba bien. José podía sentir que algo andaba mal pero no sabía qué.

El jefe hechicero empezó a hablar:

- Hoy es el día en que le entregaré mi puesto como jefe a Jo...

- ¡CLASH! Una hechicera malvada salió de un agujero en el techo.

- ¡Mario, detente! -interrumpió la hechicera malvada antes de que el jefe hechicero terminara de hablar. Otros dos malvados secuaces brincaron del agujero en el techo. Los dos hicieron un círculo alrededor del jefe, con la hechicera malvada en el medio.

El viejo hechicero miró a José mientras apuntaba hacia el portal con la cabeza. José suspiró profundamente mientras más secuaces salían del agujero. Se bajó de su silla y empezó a gatear hacia el portal. Miró a los hechiceros y hechiceras chicos, y haciendo un gesto con las manos, los llamó susurrando- "Vengan para acá"

Los chicos empezaron a gatear hacia José, brincando todos en el portal y de último entró José.

Aterrizaron frente a una escuela con ropa diferente. Una mujer abría las puertas.

- ¿Es usted el Sr. José, el sustituto y los estudiantes de intercambio?

- Ahhh...¡Sí! -dijo José.

- Ok, venga para acá -dijo la mujer -esta es su clase, si necesita algo estoy en la habitación número 125 al final del pasillo.

José estaba muy confundido. - Oh, y si tiene problemas con un estudiante, solo me lo manda a la oficina. Yo soy la directora Nancy- dijo-mientras abría la puerta.

- Estudiantes, la Sra. Gibson se encuentra en un hospital en Brasil cuidando a unos niños. Este es su sustituto, el Sr. José.

La directora Nancy miró a José. – En su escritorio hay un horario con lo que tiene que hacer el día de hoy.

Luego miró a los estudiantes de cuarto grado otra vez. - Y estos niños son los estudiantes de intercambio.

Los chicos y chicas hechiceros, observaron la clase. - Sean buenos con el Sr. José -dijo la directora Nancy, y luego camino hacia su oficina.

Los estudiantes de cuarto grado esperaron pacientemente mientras el Sr. José y los supuestos estudiantes de intercambio hablaban en el pasillo.

- Ok, ustedes se van a sentar en las sillas y yo voy a hacer lo que me dice el calendario -susurró José a los hechiceros y hechiceras chicos.

- Ok -respondieron los chicos.

Uno de los chicos hechiceros vio a otro niño que estaba jugando con su chicle. Tenía los ojos cerrados y estaba sentado en una silla que no era de él. El joven hechicero cerró los ojos y con las manos apuntó al niño. ¡Zap! Magia verde le salió de las manos y llego a donde estaba el niño sentado. Este flotó por el aire hacia otra silla que estaba vacía.

Nadie vio esto, excepto José, porque el niño estaba sentado en la fila de atrás. José miró al joven hechicero con una cara que decía "en serio.. no hagas eso".

Luego, José se concentró en el horario que decía "Primero presente a los estudiantes de intercambio" - Ok -pensó.

Para entonces, el niño que estaba jugando con su chicle abrió los ojos. Estaba confundido - ¿Estaba yo sentado aquí antes? -Pensó el niño, se encogió de hombros y cerró sus ojos otra vez.

- Ok hechiceros y hechiceras vengan para acá -dijo José. Todos los estudiantes de cuarto grado estaban confundidos.

- Yo soy Estrella -dijo una chica hechicera.

- Yo soy Arbolito -dijo un chico hechicero.

- Yo soy Chiquilla -dijo otra chica hechicera.

- Yo soy Envolverno -dijo un chico hechicero.

- Yo soy Quemarela -dijo una hechicera pequeña.

- Yo soy Auguaito -dijo el último hechicero pequeño.

- Y yo soy Clima -dijo la última hechicera.

Los estudiantes estaban muy confundidos porque estos nombres eran también nombres de cosas, por ejemplo: Estrella. Todos los estudiantes pensaron que tal vez estos estudiantes de intercambio venían de otro lugar donde a los niños se le ponen nombres así, porque si no, algo sospechoso estaba pasando.

- Ok, gracias -dijo José. Regresen a sus asientos. Todos los hechiceros y hechiceras caminaron hacia sus sillas.

Luego, era hora de estudiar la lección en ciencias. -el calendario dice que tenemos que estudiar la lección sobre "centavos de bronce, plata y oro" -leyó el Sr. José. – (que es un experimento químico con centavos de dólar que los niños aprenden en cuarto grado, pero él no sabía eso)

Ok -dijo el Sr. José, -centavos de bronce, plata y oro-.

Una niña se paró y le dijo -Sr. José, yo soy Miliani, los mecheros de bunsen están en el closet y las monedas están en el cajón.

José no sabía de qué estaba hablando Miliani, pero dijo – "Envolverno, ven acá". José susurró algo en la oreja de Envolverno y él salió de la clase corriendo muy rápido. En sólo 30 segundos regresó con las manos llenas de monedas.

- ¿Puedes dárselas a tus compañeros por favor? -preguntó el Sr. José a Envolverno. Envolverno le entregó una moneda a cada uno.

- Ahora dice que hay que quemarlas ¿Puedes quemar las monedas por favor? -preguntó el Sr. José a Quemarela quien caminó por todos los escritorios soplando las monedas. Todas las monedas empezaron a quemarse frente a ellos.

Todo el día hicieron cosas muy extrañas, la forma mágica para resolver matemáticas, para estudios sociales, para leer, para escritura y para todas las demás cosas que haces en escuela, incluyendo el recreo.

Cuando los estudiantes regresaron a sus casas les contaron a sus padres todo lo que hicieron en clase. Los papás pensaron que estaban bromeando. Pero en pocas semanas los estudiantes comenzaron a aprender cómo hacer magia.

Un día, cuando supo que ya era hora, el Sr. José les comunicó esta gran noticia a sus estudiantes. – "Necesitamos prepararnos para la batalla" –

José les contó a sus estudiantes su verdadera historia. Todos los niños se organizaron en grupos donde siempre hubo un estudiante hechicero. Todos los grupos eran expertos en las cosas que tendrían que hacer.

Finalmente llegó el momento. Todos formaron un círculo. -El grupo Chiquilla tendría que encogerse para entrar en la cerradura y desbloquearla. Después, había que distraer a la hechicera y a sus secuaces. El grupo Quemarela, debía a rescatar a los demás hechiceros y hechiceras que están en el calabozo, y todos los demás debían luchar juntos, excepto el grupo

Clima -explico el Sr. José.

Todos hicieron su trabajo, el grupo Chiquilla desbloqueó la puerta y distrajo a la hechicera y a sus ayudantes, el grupo Quemarela rescató a las hechiceras y hechiceros, los otros grupos pelearon juntos y el grupo Clima hizo llover y provocó estruendos para la batalla.

Y claro, ganaron.

Después de la victoria, el jefe hechicero organizó una ceremonia de entrega de premios.

- Esto es para ti José, una medalla y tú vas a ser el nuevo jefe hechicero -dijo el viejo jefe hechicero que se llamaba Mario.

- Gracias por la medalla pero yo no deseo ser jefe -dijo José. -Yo quiero estar con estos niños, pero no enseñando magia, sino de la manera correcta, a la manera humana.

Todos los estudiantes corrieron hacia el Sr. Márquez y le dieron un abrazo.

-Nos gusta mucho más que seas nuestro maestro en South West Community Campus -dijo una niña que se llama Mercedes. Todos los otros estudiantes pensaban lo mismo.

- Ok, yo voy a nombrar como jefe a alguien más. Pero tú necesitas tener un nombre y un apellido, ya todos los maestros usan sus apellidos. Además, los chicos y las chicas hechiceros tienen mi permiso de estar contigo también, pero necesitan usar otros nombres -dijo el jefe hechicero.

- Yo quiero ser Génesis -dijo Chiquilla.

- Yo quiero ser Eduardo -dijo Arbolito.

- Yo quiero ser Yerik -dijo Envolverno.

- Yo quiero ser Samayah, No Aaminah. Sí, yo quiero Aaminah -dijo Clima.

- Yo voy a ser Katy -dijo Quemarela.

- Yo voy a ser Remi -dijo Auguaito.

- Y yo voy a ser Harper -dijo Estrella.

- Yo voy a ser José Márquez -dijo José.

Así es como José termino trabajando en el South West Community Campus por mucho tiempo, usando la manera humana de enseñar. La Sra. Gibson se mudó a primer grado y el equipo del Sr. Márquez ganó la batalla.

El señor Márquez terminó de contar la historia diciendo- A los estudiantes les encanta ver a José todos los días y ahora me dicen Sr. Márquez."

Un niño que se llama Alan dijo- Yo conozco a Harper, ella está en quinto grado y tú... eres José Márquez.

- Sí, y esta es la historia de mi vida -replicó el Sr. Márquez sonriendo.

About the Author

Harper Davis has written many stories that she has shared with her family and friends. She also writes and performs plays and musicals with her sister Kyle and cousins, Evie and Lincoln. One interesting thing about Harper is that she had brain surgery in first grade, 2017. Harper is currently in 4th grade at SouthWest Community Campus, a bilingual school in Grand Rapids MI. She loves cooking, baking, singing, dancing, drawing, writing stories, plays, and songs. She also likes doing crafts. Harper loves seeing musicals. She has a puppy, Calvin, and 3 siblings: her little sister Kyle, her brother Ford, and her littlest sister Margie.

Spanish Language - Youth Published Finalist

La princesa del mar
Anja Phillips

Capítulo 1 Una Reina

Había una vez una princesa llamada Cora que quería ser reina del mar. Ella no podía ser reina porque tenía una hermana mayor. Su hermana mayor se llamaba Lily y estaba emocionada por la ceremonia que haría la reina.

Un día, la mamá de Cora le dijo -cuando tu hermana no esté, tú serás la reina-. Cora estaba emocionada y se lo contó a su hermana mayor, pero cuando Lili escuchó lo que Cora le dijo no se puso muy feliz. Enojada, Lili corrió hasta su mamá y le preguntó- ¿Por qué le dijiste que Cora podía ser reina cuando yo no estoy? La mamá dijo -si tú no estás, entonces no habrá reina, allí es cuando yo le dije a Cora que podía ser reina.

Finalmente era tiempo para la coronación de la nueva reina Lily, la hermana mayor de Cora. Todos estaban felices y decían -Buen trabajo Reina Lily. ¡Ese día hubo una gran fiesta! Todos estaban allí, había muchos juegos y comida deliciosa. Fue muy divertido. Cora y su hermana estaban muy contentas.

La pequeña ciudad tenía nuevas leyes:

1. No tirar basura.
2. Tratar bien a todos.
3. Ir a escuela y no ir a la escuela cuando estés enfermo.
4. Jugar con todos.
5. Obedecer a tus padres.

Estas eran las leyes nuevas. A todo el pueblo le gustaban las nuevas leyes.

Unos meses pasaron y la reina se fue de viaje. Cora olvidó lo que su madre le había dicho.

Todas las personas estaban haciendo muchas cosas como si no tuvieran una reina. En este momento Cora recordó lo que su madre le había dicho. Ella se sentó en el trono de la reina y dijo:

- Recuerden, siempre hay una reina.

Cuando la reina Lily regresó, Cora dijo -¡Yo voy a ser la reina del jardín! Todos dijeron que sí porque nadie va allí para darle agua a las plantas y a las flores. La hermana de Cora compró lo que necesitó durante el viaje.

Cora quería hacer un baile de gala e invitó a todas sus amigas. Todas dijeron, -¡Tú eres la reina del jardín ahora! Esa noche hubo un baile de gala. Todos estaban allí bailando.

Unas semanas después, Cora dijo con tristeza- No hay nadie aquí. –

La Reina Lily dijo - es porque yo soy reina y no hay nadie aquí en el jardín. Cora dijo -entonces yo no voy ser reina del jardín.

Pero Lily dijo- No, todavía puedes ser reina del jardín. –

Pero Cora ya no quería ser reina del jardín. Así que se fue al pueblo para ver a sus amigas Ava, Harper y Addy y divertirse con ellas. Cuando ellas estaban jugando, Cora encontró un animal mágico.

§

Capítulo 2

La Gata Mágica

Cora y sus amigas encontraron una gata mágica. No es fácil encontrar una gata mágica. Ellas querían llamarle Ela. Era hermosa pero no podía encontrar a su familia.

Cora decidió cuidar de Ela en el palacio con sus amigas. Era difícil pero lo hizo. Ellas le hicieron una cama y le pusieron platos y tazas para comer y tomar leche. Era difícil porque era mágica.

Cora le dijo a la gata mágica -¡Tú y yo vamos a encontrar a tu familia, ahora!

Pero la gata mágica estaba triste porque amaba a Cora y Cora también la amaba a ella. Entre todas, encontraron a la familia de la gata mágica.

Cuando Cora estaba en el palacio escuchó algo. Ella vio que era la gata mágica, Ela había decidido vivir en el palacio con Cora, la princesa del mar. Fin.

About the Author

Anja Phillips is a third grader who lives with her mom, dad, older brother and younger sister in Holland, MI. She is in a Spanish Immersion program at her school. She loves to play with her friends and siblings. She has a great imagination and loves to create stories, drawings and crafts. She also loves to explore the great outdoors.

Spanish Language - Youth Published Finalist

Historia contra historia
Alivia Schnakenberg

En una granja pequeña y hermosa en México, vivían unos hermanos, Ana y Luis.

Los dos niños eran pobres y sólo tenían diez pesos. No se puede vivir en México solo con diez pesos, por eso era necesario para sus padres conseguir trabajo, así que se fueron en un barco viejo y oxidado que tenían, buscando un lugar donde trabajar. El barco no era el mejor pero era el único transporte que su familia poseía. Estas son las historias de todo lo que le pasó a esta familia.

Poco tiempo después encontraron trabajo y se volvieron ricos, gozaban de mucho dinero y una casa enorme. Ana y Luis podían hacer todo lo que querían y no tenían ni una preocupación. Vivían felices con sus barrigas llenas de comida, sus armarios llenos de ropa y sus mentes llenos de sueños.

Pero un día todo cambió. Todos estaban durmiendo en sus cómodas camas cuando de repente se despertaron al sonido de la alarma de fuego; habían olvidado la estufa encendida. Aunque toda la familia escapó y se pusieron a salvo, sus riquezas se convirtieron en cenizas.

Un poco después, Ana y Luis estaban cultivando su huerto cuando escucharon música en la calle. Los dos gemelos gritaron ¡Helado! Mientras corrían, pero Luis recordó que no tenía mucho dinero. Ambos estaban tristes caminando de regreso a su verde y pequeño jardín, cuando Luis vio un papel que volaba desde la calle. Frustrado lo levantó y se quejó- Este es el quinto papel que recojo hoy.

- ¿Puedo verlo? -dijo Ana.

- Sí, no tiene nada importante.

- ¡Mira! Dice que podemos ir a este lugar en la Avenida Juárez y contar una historia de la vida real para ganar un premio- observó Ana emocionada.

- ¿Ganar qué Ana?

- ¡CIEN MIL PESOS! -gritó Ana muy emocionada.

Los dos niños caminaron hacia la Avenida Juárez y allí le contaron la historia del incendio de su casa a una mujer, quien escribió todo en un papel y lo puso en un sobre.

- Entreguen este sobre al hombre con bigote ancho y de color marrón a quien encontrarán en la tienda de telescopios.

- Gracias por ayudarnos -le susurraron los gemelos- y caminaron rápidamente a la tienda de telescopios.

Cuando entraron a la tienda, miraron alrededor y vieron muchísimos telescopios. Había algunos altos y otros más bajos, algunos con muchos colores y otros sin mucho color. Luis buscaba al hombre del bigote peludo mientras Ana miraba un telescopio enorme y muy poderoso.

- ¿Quiénes son ustedes? – preguntó el hombre con bigote ancho y marrón.

- Ana susurró - Solo somos mi hermano y yo.

- El hombre se dio la vuelta y gritó como si fuera un león muy enojado -¡No toquen mis telescopios!-

- Solo queríamos entregarle esta historia -dijo Luis en voz alta-.

- El Señor con el bigote les preguntó -¿Y los 20 pesos?

Los gemelos estaban tan confundidos como una zebra en el océano. Ana iba a contestar que no necesitaban pagar dinero pero Luis sacó el papel y lo revisó nuevamente. En el papel decía que necesitaban pagar veinte pesos si querían entrar a la competencia. Ellos solo tenían diez pesos. Los gemelos caminaron dos millas largas para regresar a su casa mientras discutían qué harían para ganarse veinte pesos.

Ana pensó que podían encontrar a alguien interesado en historias que pudiera pagar veinte pesos. Cuando finalmente regresaron a su casa en la noche sus padres no estaban allí, así que tuvieron que dormir sin ellos.

Cuando despertaron se fueron a la tienda otra vez y la misma mujer que les escribió la historia les ayudó nuevamente, esta vez con una fábula. Ya después se toparon con un niño que quería comprar una historia. Él les pagó dos billetes de diez dólares. Los niños, emocionados fueron a un banco para asegurarse de que los billetes eran reales, pero la cajera tiró uno en la basura - ¿Por qué ha hecho esto? –Gritó a ambos niños al mismo tiempo, -Este peso es falso – contestó la cajera.

Los niños continuaron contando e inventando historias que luego vendían, hasta que consiguieron los pesos que necesitaban. Una vez que pagaron para el concurso, el juez les dijo -Les daré los resultados el viernes a las nueve.

- ¡Gracias!- respondieron emocionados los gemelos que no podían creer que habían entrado a la competencia.

Los gemelos regresaron a su vieja casa por la noche y se alegraron de que sus padres habían regresado también. Por la noche, Ana y Luis les contaron qué pasó cuando ellos no estaban y sus padres les contaron que seguían sin encontrar un trabajo. Pero todos estaban contentos de estar juntos y porque muy pronto sería viernes.

Cuando todos despertaron tenían muchísima hambre y se podía escuchar sus estómagos como un elefante en la jungla. No tenían mucho para comer, entonces Ana se fue al bosque para buscar un mango, una papaya, un aguacate y finalmente un mamey. Cuando ella entró en el bosque encontró todas las frutas que necesitaba. El mango se veía como un arcoíris, la papaya tenía un buen olor, el aguacate se veía perfecto y finalmente el mamey se sentía como un aguacate maduro.

Ese día, jueves, tuvieron que trabajar mucho en su casa. Su mamá cultivó el jardín, papá trató de encontrar un trabajo y Luis le ayudó a Mamá a limpiar todas las cosas que tenían en su casa (aunque no había mucho). Al final del día, todos estaban cansados y querían dormir, entonces se comieron el mango y fueron a dormir. Todos estaban muy felices porque habían trabajado mucho ese día.

Ana y Luis se despertaron muy temprano en la mañana para ir a preguntar quién ganó la competencia de historias. Los dos hermanos corrieron como un leopardo para llegar a tiempo. Había algunos jueces reunidos discutiendo sobre las historias y finalmente el juez anunció – Damas y caballeros, niños y niñas, hemos recibido un total de 2063 historias. El tercer lugar es para Jorge, el segundo lugar es para la Señora Leah y el primer lugar se le otorga a... ¡Ana y Luis!

Todas las personas quienes ganaron, caminaban con orgullo como si fueran reyes y reinas frente a los jueces y recibieron todo el dinero del premio, mientras toda la audiencia los aplaudía como si fueran truenos que nunca se paraban. Los gemelos tomaron el dinero y corrieron a su casa lo más rápido posible. Cuando llegaron, su papá tomó el dinero y después de algunas semanas, todos se mudaron a su nueva casa. Era mejor, más bonita y más grande que su casa del pasado.

Los gemelos tenían camas reales, encontraron una casa pequeña que hicieron suya y siempre disfrutaron de su familia. Finalmente, donaron algo de dinero a todas las personas pobres que lo necesitaban para vivir felices también ellos.

Fin.

About the Author

Alivia was born in Michigan and has lived there her whole life. She feels blessed to be in the Spanish Immersion program at her school. In her spare time, she likes playing the piano, twisting balloon animals, gardening, and raising Monarch butterflies during the summer. When she grows up, she hopes to be a teacher or have a job that helps kids.

About Write Michigan

The Write Michigan Short Story contest began in 2012 as a dream. Kent District Library Director Lance Werner envisioned libraries and publishers working together to highlight the efforts of Michigan writers via an independently published book. What better way to engage readers and writers than a writing contest? Writers could create a short story; readers could read those short stories. Nearly 600 writers from all over the state entered the inaugural contest. Author Wade Rouse contributed the foreword to the first anthology.

For the ninth annual contest, KDL, Schuler Books and new partner, Hancock School Public Library received submissions from across the state of Michigan, including the Upper Peninsula. The contest garnered almost 1,000 entries, and 160 reviewers narrowed the field to ten semifinalists in each category. Eight judges (including some of last year's winners) determined the Judges' Choice and Runner-Up winners. Public votes determined the Readers' Choice winner in each category. Cash prizes amounting to $5,000 were distributed during the award ceremony. Author Susie Finkbeiner offered both the award ceremony keynote address and the foreword to the Write Michigan 2021 Anthology.

The Write Michigan Short Story Contest has established itself as a premier writing contest in the Mitten State. Libraries and bookstores share the goal of fueling interest in libraries, writing and reading. The Write Michigan Short Story Contest is an integral part of that goal.

2021 Judges

Adult Category

DAN JOHNSON

Dan Johnson is the author (as D.E. Johnson) of the Will Anderson Detroit Mysteries, which include The Detroit Electric Scheme, Motor City Shakedown, Detroit Breakdown, and Detroit Shuffle, which were published by St. Martin's Minotaur Books. He is a two-time winner of the Michigan Notable Book Award. Dan lives south of Kalamazoo with his lovely and talented wife and a less lovely and talented pair of cats.

SHELLEY IRWIN

Shelley Irwin is the host and producer for The WGVU Morning Show, a newsmagazine talk-show format on the local NPR affiliate Monday through Friday. The show, broadcast from 9 a.m. to 11 a.m. features a wide variety of local and national newsmakers, plus special features. She also hosts several public affairs program on the TV side, including Family Health Matters and Kalamazoo Lively Arts. Shelley is award winning in her profession, including five consecutive Gracie Allen Awards from American Women in TV and Radio for excellence as a program host. She was awarded the 2016 Athena Award, honoring an individual who has demonstrated leadership in their profession, mentored and opened new opportunities for women and contributed time and talent to the community and the Rotary of Grand Rapids' Service Above Self award, given in recognition of Frederik Meijer, whose humanitarian acts of selfless service made an enduring difference in the lives of others. Most recently, Irwin was named as one of the 200 Most Powerful Business Leaders in West Michigan by the Grand Rapids Business Journal. Her community involvement extends from the Kent County Park Foundation to the Michigan Women's Foundation, Hope Network, Girl Scouts and the Cherry Health Foundation, among others. She has been named one of the "50 Most Influential Women in West Michigan" twice by Gemini Publications, and has represented the U.S. in the Long Distance Triathlon and Duathlon World Championships.

Teen Category

ANJA VAN DRUNEN

Anja Van Drunen is a young Christian writer. When she isn't happily arguing with imaginary people while hunched over a keyboard and drinking mango tea, she's listening to educational podcasts, enjoying yet another adaptation of the Sherlock Holmes stories, or debating obscure points of English syntax (in between homework assignments, of course). You can reach her at writingvandrunen@gmail.com.

MICHELLE KASTANEK

Michelle M. Kastanek lives in Alto, Michigan with her husband, Cody, and cat (more affectionately referred to as "shat"), Aravis. A fantasy writer, she as been described as one with an "unusual mind," and enjoys living up to that expectation. A combination of cat cuddles from Aravis, a cup of tea (or wine), and classical music is her recipe for a productive writing session. But more often, she writes to the sound of Office episodes and unending questions from her husband while eating raw cookie dough.

When not writing (or working her big-girl job), Kastanek can be found traveling the world (don't ask her favorite destination – she doesn't know), playing board games, cuddling with a good book, or helping to run her family business, The Comic Signal.

Website: mmkastanek.weebly.com | Instagram: @mmkastanek

Youth

DEBORAH DIESEN

Deborah Diesen is the author of many children's picture books, including Equality's Call: The Story of Voting Rights in America and the NYT-bestselling The Pout-Pout Fish. She has worked as a bookseller, a bookkeeper, and a reference librarian. She and her family live in Michigan.

RAMONA WILKE

My name is Ramona Wilke, and I am almost 13 years old. I grew up in west Michigan with my parents and two younger brothers. Last year I was the runner-up for judges choice in the youth category of the Write Michigan contest. I have always enjoyed writing fictional stories and plan to do so in my future.

Spanish-Language Youth

RAMON PERALTA

My name is Ramón Peralta, I'm from the Dominican Republic and I have been living in Grand Rapids since 1982. My education: Bachelor's degree in Philosophy and History (University of Santo Domingo), a Master's degree in History (Michigan State University). I'm a co-author of two books: "Azucar, Encomiendas y otros Ensayos Históricos" (1979) and "Religión, Filosofía y Política en Fernando A. de Meriño, 1857-1906" (1979). I was a professor of Dominican History in the University of Santo Domingo. In Grand Rapids I worked for 26 years in Grand Rapids Public School in Adult Education and as a Family Support Specialist at the main office of GRPS. I have been a columnist for 28 years in "El Vocero Hispano," a Hispanic newspaper in Grand Rapids. Right now I'm retired.

GLORIA TREJO

Gloria Trejo es una Abogado y Pedagoga mexicana, a su vez que una Escritora, Poeta y columnista originaria de Rio Bravo, Tamaulipas, Mexico. Colaboró con el periódico "LA VOZ HISPANA DE NUEVA YORK" Newspaper con la columna semanal "ALMA DE MUJER". Forma parte de Lucia Macias Theater Company, como autora. Obras de teatro "CINCO DE MAYO", "POETA YO", "SOÑANDO CON FRIDA". Es Miembro de movimiento cultural "Mujeres poetas Internacional" donde colabora con el Movimiento "GRITO DE MUJER" y autora de "A ti mujer" poema para la respectiva Antología Poética. Colaboró tambien en la Antología poética chilena "POR QUE MEXICO?". De igual manera colaboró en Antología poética chilena dedicada a Federico Garcia Lorca. Ganadora del Primer Concurso de Poesía de QM Editorial, con el poema "ANDABA BUSCANDO UN POEMA". Ha publicado, de su autoría, el libro de poemas "CONTEMPLO ESTRELLAS: Donde la fe y el amor a la vida se imponen". De igual manera, el libro de cuentos infantiles "LLUEVE CHOCOLATE", obra de carácter didáctico resalta los valores y principios Universales donde el niño y la naturaleza juegan un rol principal. Gloria Trejo es voluntaria de Grand Rapids Public School. Actualmente colabora en el area cultural con la Comunidad de South West de Grand Rapids, tratando de suplir las necesidades de la Comunidad latina en el área de la lecto- escritura del idioma Español por medio de diversas disciplinas artisticas. E igualmente trabajando con las mujeres con su Taller de Literaterapia.

Gloria Trejo is a Mexican lawyer and educator, as well as a writer, poet and columnist from Rio Bravo, Tamaulipas, Mexico. She collaborated with the newspaper "LA VOZ HISPANA DE NUEVA YORK" Newspaper with the weekly column "ALMA DE MUJER". She is part of Lucia Macias Theater Company, as the author. Her theater plays include "CINCO DE MAYO", "POETA YO", and "DREAMING WITH FRIDA". She is a member of the cultural movement "Mujeres poetas, Internacional" where she collaborates with the "GRITO DE MUJER" Movement and author of "A ti mujer" poem for the respective Poetic Anthology. She also collaborated in the Chilean Poetic Anthology "POR QUE MEXICO?". She likewise collaborated in the Chilean Poetic Anthology dedicated to Federico Garcia Lorca. She was the winner of the First QM Editorial Poetry Contest, with the poem "I WAS LOOKING FOR A POEM". She has authored and published the book of poems "CONTEMPLATING STARS: Where faith and love of life are imposed". Similarly, her children's story book "RAIN CHOCOLATE" is a didactic work that highlights the universal values and principles where the child and nature play a main role. Gloria Trejo is a Grand Rapids Public School volunteer. She currently collaborates in the cultural area with the Community of the South West of Grand Rapids, trying to meet the needs of the Latino Community in the area of reading and writing the Spanish language through various artistic disciplines. She is also working with women with her Literatherapy Workshop.

Acknowledgements

Once again, Write Michigan has attracted terrific authors from all age groups and across the state. With nearly 1,000 entries, it's challenging to select only a few for publishing in this anthology.

Write Michigan is made possible by the 160 volunteers who reviewed the entries received this year. And what would we do without our judges? Deborah Diesen, Shelley Irwin, Dan Johnson, Michelle Kastanek, Ramón Peralta, Deborah Reed, Gloria Trejo, Anja Van Drunen and Ramona Wilke each poured a part of themselves into this contest and for that we are grateful beyond words.

Our heartfelt gratitude goes to Susie Finkbeiner for her support by writing the Foreword to this book, as well as delivering the keynote address at the Write Michigan Short Story Contest Awards Ceremony.

We are sincerely grateful for the generous support of Meijer, Kent District Library and Schuler Books as sponsors. We are thrilled to welcome Hancock School Public Library as a new partner this year.

Thanks also to the Write Michigan Committee for organizing and promoting the short story contest: Brad Baker, Diane Cutler, Randy Goble, Julia Hawkins, Sara Proano, David Specht, Remington Steed and Katie Zuidema. Their attention to detail and can-do attitude make this huge project seem easy.

Lance Werner, Executive Director of Kent District Library, and Bill and Cecile Fehsenfeld, owners of Schuler Books, are terrific champions of this project.

Finally, it is **you**, our readers, who deserve thanks for participating in Write Michigan by reading and rating entries, telling others about the contest, visiting libraries around the state and encouraging writers to put their words on paper to make their voices heard.

Kip Odell, Kent District Library

Pierre Camy, Schuler Books

Sponsors

meijer®

SCHULER BOOKS

HANCOCK SCHOOL
PUBLIC LIBRARY

Kent
District
Library

kdl.org

Self-Publishing Services

Thanks to Schuler Books' Espresso Book Machine, we can help you print your book. You provide us with two PDF files (one for the cover and one for the text or bookblock) and we will print a high-quality paperback book for you, in color or black and white. The Espresso Book Machine can print books from 40 pages to 650 pages long.

What are the benefits of printing your work with Schuler Books?

* This is your book.
* You'll receive one-on-one support
* Since you sign a non-exclusive contract with us, you may pursue any other publishing venture that you choose.
* You retain all rights to the printed work, and you have complete control over layout, content and design.
* No minimums. You may print one copy or as many as you want.
* You retain rights for non-exclusive distribution and may sell books printed at Schuler Books or with the Chapbook Press through any avenue.
* Modifications are allowed at any time, for an additional fee.
* You set the book price and determine the royalty per book.

What we need to print your book

2 print-ready PDF files: one for the book and one for the cover, formatted the way you want them to look. We will upload your files and print a paperback edition of your book on high quality (archival) paper and a full-color glossy cover, in any size you want from 5"x 5" to around 8" x 10.5"

We can help you get there

We can help as much or as little as needed in each area of making your book a reality.

New Services:

* eBook /Global distribution print and digital package: Your title (in print or as an eBook) will be available for purchase to over 39,000 global retailers, and their customers. The eBook will be available for more than 70 different eReaders including Amazon Kindle, Apple iBookstore, Barnes&Noble NOOK, Kobo, Sony, etc.) Bookstores and retailers around the world will be able to order your book for their customers.
* Title set-up:
    * Book and e-book: $750 ($800 if book interior is in color)—includes 2 ISBNs
    * Book only: $620 ($670 if book interior is in color)—includes 1 ISBN

You need to order a minimum of 50 copies within 60 days of title set-up.
Additional orders (minimum quantity of 10), require a three week notice.

* Epub Conversion: $1 per page (page count is based on the total number of pages in your bookblock)
    * Conversion will take three weeks.
    * For Printing costs and author compensation please ask for a quote.

Chapbook Press

	Short Run	Standard Package	Chapbook Press Publishing
	$60 Plus Production Costs	**$180** Plus Production Costs	**$360** Plus Production Costs
Maximum Print Run	20 Copies	Unlimited	Unlimited
Page Maximum	100 Pages	650 Pages	650 Pages
Personal Consultation	30 Minutes	30 Minutes	60 Minutes
Email Support	Limited Support	Included	Included
PDF Review	No	No	Yes
Proof Copy	1 Proof Copy	1 Proof Copy	1 Proof Copy
PDF Upload	Includes initial upload No Re-uploads	Includes initial upload +1 Re-upload	Includes initial upload +1 Re-upload
Cover	Basic Text Cover	Basic Template Cover	Basic Template Cover
Saved for Re-prints	No	Yes	Yes
ISBN/Barcode	No	No	Yes
Library of Congress Reg.	No	No	Yes
Books in Print Reg.	No	No	Yes
Sale: Schuler Books	No	No	Yes
Sale: SchulerBooks.com	No	No	Yes
Production Costs	**$8.00 per copy** flat rate	**$7.00 per copy** +$0.03 per page	**$7.00 per copy** +$0.03 per page
Color Interior	No	+$0.15 per page	+$0.15 per page

A la Carte Sevices

Transcribing: $126 deposit, $42 per hour
Coaching/Consulting: $60 deposit, $60 per hour
Manuscript evaluation: $300
Content/Copy Editing: $54 per hour, $162 deposit
Proofreading: $126 deposit, $42 per hour
Scanning: $60 deposit, $60 per hour
Page Layout: $120 deposit, $60 per hour
Custom Cover Design: $120 deposit, $60 per hour

PDF Alterations (re-uploads)**:** $35 (+ price of proof copy)
Cover from Template: $60 (prepay)
ISBN & barcode acquisition: $120
Amazon listing: $60
Library of Congress Registration: $60
Additional consultation time: $50 per hour
Manuscript editing: $162 deposit, $54 per hour
Hardcover Binding: Ask for a quote.

For more information visit SchulerBooks.com
Want to talk to someone? Call us today at 616-942-7330 x 558,
or email us at: printondemand@schulerbooks.com